More Than Money
...a police novel

By

D. Clayton Mayes

5/21/04

Jim
Thank you!
for all your help!
your professional
work is worth
"More than Money"
thank you
Clayton

ISBN: 1-4033-0701-6 (e-book)
ISBN: 1-4033-0702-4 (Paperback)
ISBN: 1-4033-0703-2 (Dustjacket)

This book is printed on acid free paper.

This fictional work represents the author's creation through January, 2002.

1stBooks - rev. 07/12/02

ACKNOWLEDGMENTS

I would like to acknowledge the assistance and help offered to me in the creation of the novel. I am extremely appreciative for the constructive criticism given by my family, friends and fellow officers. I would especially like to thank my friend Gail Hopke for her insight and encouragement in getting this book published. And also Erman Pessis for his kind assistance and suggestions.

To my wife, Carolyn, a very special "thank you." Without your help, support and steadfast love, this book would not have been possible.

INTRODUCTION

All successful people have at least three things in common. They are goal oriented, have a deep sense of responsibility and a positive self-image. For "street-cops," that is not enough. Survival is the goal. They must go to work, stay alive and go home at "end of watch." Like clockwork, every two weeks they collect their paycheck. Actually, it is pretty simple, unless one is like Brad Phillips, where his work is a "Labor of Love."

A successful baseball player, corporate executive or concert director has to love his or her work to be successful. They have to put their heart into their work. Successful cops have to do the same. Often they don't achieve the proper balance in their lives. Their values can become distorted and corrupt them.

The decisions that a cop has to make daily are mind-boggling. In a gunfight it is "shoot, shoot or be shot." They must make the decision to pull the trigger one-tenth of an inch in one-tenth of a second and that decision may very well haunt the officer for the rest of his life. Often reviewed for more than ten months, the Supreme Court cannot even agree on the decision the officer should have made. The cop doesn't get a second chance to consider his decision over a ten-month period. It is life or death at that moment, at least in their mind.

Peer pressure plays an important role in the environment they work in. Cops are pretty good at keeping their emotional pain inside. Nevertheless, the pain is branded deep inside their mind and soul.

Police recruiters have identified responsibility, honor and action as the prime motivators that attract men and women to police work, but money makes the real world turn. What can be worth more than money? Where do honesty, integrity and courage fit in the scheme of things? Like most cops, Brad Phillips had to weigh these matters.

Would confronting a nut with a briefcase full of dynamite or waving a hand grenade at you change your value system? Where does dope fit in the equation? How much money would it take to turn a good cop into a bad cop? Join Brad Phillips on a walk through life from his perspective.

TABLE OF CONTENTS

Acknowledgments..iii

Introduction...v

Chapter 1:   Man Stole A Gun 1

Chapter 2:   Take The Right Turn..................................... 10

Chapter 3:   Meet The Teacher 20

Chapter 4:   Weekend Warrior... 33

Chapter 5:   Traffic.. 44

Chapter 6:   Go To The Station.. 57

Chapter 7:   Street Cops 64

Chapter 8:   Walking The Beat 78

Chapter 9:   The Vice 100

Chapter 10: Kiddy Cops 113

Chapter 11: Silver Tongue.. 129

Chapter 12: The Bicentennial 141

Chapter 13: Fit Or Unfit?... 150

Chapter 14: Dopey 157

Chapter 15: Found Property.. 171

Chapter 16: Officer Needs Help 179

1

MAN STOLE A GUN

It was a February afternoon. I was working the day watch in an "L" unit, a one-officer car, when I picked up the microphone and cleared from my last radio call. I glanced at my watch and saw it was 3:40 p.m. I thought, if I could only make it five more minutes without getting another radio call, I would get off work a little early or at least on time. As I was attending college three nights a week, my hands were full enough without having to work overtime.

While there was snow on the ground in the northeastern states, it was hot and smoggy in Los Angeles. After eight hours in an LAPD uniform, my body told me I needed a shower. My mind said I was getting tired but my stomach growled; I needed to eat again.

Most of the day watch units had already headed for the station as the night watch would hit the streets a little early, around 3:45 p.m. This would allow the day watch to go end of watch about fifteen minutes early. The night watch lieutenant was a "good guy," considerate of the officers who had been working for eight hours.

Suddenly, my radio sounded with a high tone, followed by the link operator's distinct voice, "Any unit in the vicinity of 14th and Olive Avenue, at Wade's Gun Store, a theft just occurred; man stole a gun. Any unit identify and handle the call Code 2."

"Oh nuts!" I muttered to myself. If I only waited a minute longer before clearing from my last assignment, I would have made it to school on time or at least nearly on time. Obviously, the more seasoned veterans of the street knew better than to clear so eagerly.

By the time the operator repeated the call, I could see that no other unit was going to volunteer to take the call. If a unit was clear or available it would assist. I, the young rookie cop, would be assigned the call, meaning that I alone would have to do all the paperwork.

All good street cops dislike the paperwork portion of police work. Another twenty seconds and the link operator would obviously assign the call to me because I was clear, although the incident was not in my assigned district. I picked up the microphone and said, "1L1 will handle 14th and Olive and quote a twenty-minute ETA due to great distance and heavy traffic."

I had exaggerated my ETA (Estimated Time of Arrival), but it was an accepted way for Los Angeles cops to vent frustration. I was at Sunset and Alvarado when the call came out, more than four miles from 14th and Olive. 1L1 was the "north-end" car of the Old Central Division and the "downtown" cars were to handle their own districts.

After all, I had been off probation for two months now and deserved to be treated with a certain level of respect. My realization of being off probation and acknowledgment of my newly gained seniority status was giving me a boost of "ego-power."

By the time I hung the mike back on the dash board of my police car, I was inbound on the Hollywood Freeway, in 4:00 p.m. traffic, buzzing along the freeway, in and out of traffic, with my reds on, passing traffic with only a little regard for the safety of others.

As I headed for 14th Street and Olive, I remembered that several months earlier I had handled a "Man Stole A Gun" call while working with Mike Briggs on the night watch. Mike was the senior officer and he insisted that we handle the call with extreme caution. He said over and over, "Watch their hands. That's where the gun will come from and the fingers on the hands are what pull the trigger."

When we arrived at that call, we saw two men, who appeared to be drunk, on the front sidewalk arguing and punching out one another. We jumped out of the car and I realized Mike had his pistol drawn. I thought he had overreacted but he was a good training officer so I followed his lead and did the same. We approached the suspects with extreme caution and demanded that the two step back and put their hands up.

Neither suspect seemed to be armed but Mike was concerned about their hands. After we got the suspects under control, Mike patted them down. He removed a fully loaded .45 caliber automatic pistol from under the shirt of one of the suspects. The suspect had it under his shirt, tucked beneath his belt, out of sight. It was definitely a concealed weapon under California's CCW, Carrying a Concealed Weapon, laws.

We booked both of the subjects for fighting in public. The one with the loaded concealed weapon was booked for a felony. He later beat the rap when his attorney argued that the suspect's brother-in-

2

law, whom he was fighting with when we arrested him, had given him the pistol just an hour before we arrived.

The gun was a birthday gift he had received a little earlier during his thirty-eighth birthday party. Some of the guests at the party moved outside to the front yard. After a couple of hours passed and several six-packs of beer were consumed, tempers flared to the point where they got into a fistfight.

Maybe today's call would not be as complicated. In another few minutes I was exiting the southbound Harbor Freeway at 9th Street and, with a zig and a zag, was eastbound on 14th Street approaching Olive Avenue. It certainly didn't take the twenty-minutes that I gave as an ETA.

I could already see people near the intersection pointing toward the northwest corner parking lot. I followed the fingers, in a counterclockwise direction to my left, as I entered the intersection. My mind completely left the subject of getting off work on time as I approached the downtown L.A. parking lot.

Wade's Gun Store was near the southeast corner of the intersection, so if everyone was pointing toward the northwest corner, this meant that whatever had occurred had changed location by now.

As I sped into the parking lot like a knight in shining armor, I thought how lucky these people were to have me there to control the situation. As the black-and-white police car came to a skidding stop, a white '59 Chevy sped off northbound in the alley toward Olympic Boulevard. The last citizen was yelling and screaming at me as he pointed in the direction of the car. I pulled up alongside him and yelled, "Get in." The citizen, a big male, white, about thirty years old, obviously shaken up and excited, stumbled and stuttered, but finally got out that the suspects were getting away in that car and that shots had been fired at him.

At this point, a thought flashed: "Lots of paperwork on this caper!"

We chased after the vehicle as I picked up the mike and advised Communications that I was in pursuit of a white '59 Chevy with two males inside and that shots had been fired by one of the suspects.

We sped westbound on Olympic Boulevard then north on Flower Street. As the suspects ran red lights, narrowly missing cars in the busy intersections, and passed northbound traffic in the southbound lanes, we pushed with the siren blaring. I struggled to drive Code 3 with one hand and broadcast my location of pursuit over the police radio with the other hand. At the same time, I interrogated my passenger, who was as shaken up as I was, but did not hide his emotions as I had so effectively been trained to do.

By the time I reached 7th Street, my passenger had emotionally babbled that the man in the right front of the Chevy had come into the gun store and asked to see a .38 caliber revolver. The victim, a sales clerk, handed the suspect a four-inch, blue steel, Smith and Wesson Special with ten point grips. The clerk momentarily turned to get another gun from the cabinet to show him. As he turned around, he saw the suspect closing the cylinder of the revolver.

The suspect told the sales clerk that he had loaded the revolver with bullets he had brought into the store and that he was going to take the gun. The clerk did not believe the suspect and started to pursue him out of the store. As the chase began, the suspect turned and fired one shot, just missing the clerk and other passing citizens. The bullet hit the sidewalk about a foot from the clerk.

As we cleared the intersection at 6th Street and Flower, I realized that the suspects could not escape in 4:00 p.m. traffic in downtown Los Angeles. I was within one car length of their car, but they had by no means called it quits. They had blown every red light between Olympic and 6th Street, going at least fifty m.p.h., driving on the wrong side of the street, barely missing other cars, and had pedestrians running for their lives.

Just when I thought, "I've got you now," the passenger suspect turned to his left, threw his fully extended right arm over the seat and pointed his revolver directly at me. This was so clear. It was like a turret on a Sherman Tank turning to do battle with a Jeep. There was no doubt, I had obviously been mistaken. It wasn't over yet! Instinctively, I reached for my revolver.

I found it extremely difficult to drive in a pursuit at fifty m.p.h., in heavy traffic, with one hand, holding the police mike in the other hand to broadcast and at the same time point my revolver at the suspects. Actually, I was doing a poor job of all three and finally realized I would have to reorganize my strategy. I ordered my passenger, the victim, to handle the police mike. Without letting my true emotions and fear of death show, I applied the brakes gently and increased the distance between the Chevy and my black and white. I thought, certainly no one could call this a retreat, merely increasing my speed at a decreasing rate.

As the suspects turned left on 5th Street and sped westbound toward the Harbor Freeway, I retrieved the microphone from the victim, who obviously had not attended our communications procedure class. This was apparent by the link operator's persistent "1L1 - Code 1, 1L1 - Code 1." She wanted verification of my location and status.

The suspect's car took a right onto the Harbor Freeway. As he went about fifty yards down the on-ramp, he came to a skidding stop on the right shoulder to avoid rear ending the car in front of him.

As I rounded the on-ramp, I could see that the Harbor Freeway looked like a parking lot. By this time, no one was going anywhere. My heart, blood and mind were churning. Was this to be the end of my career and life?

As we skidded to stop behind and slightly to the left of the suspect's car, I yelled to my passenger, "Get behind our car and stay down." This time, I knew that my emotions were not as well concealed as twenty seconds earlier.

My eyes were still glued to the "cannon" the passenger suspect, still in his car, was pointing at me. He certainly would not hesitate to kill. He had already tried to shoot the victim, who was now hiding behind the police car. Both suspects had refused to stop as I pursued them. Maybe this was the end of the road.

Within two seconds I had put out an "Officer Needs Help" call over the radio, jumped out of the police car with my revolver drawn and taken a crouched position.

The driver of the Chevy quickly exited his car as I yelled, "Halt, or I'll shoot."

Again, my mind flashed. This suspect probably also had a gun. He had refused to stop when I pursued him. He had nearly killed people just with his driving. Now, he was still refusing to stop even when I confronted him. His partner was, without a doubt, trying to kill me. I could not see the driver's right hand, but he must have a gun in it. No doubt this would be the most justified shooting the LAPD had ever seen.

Again, I yelled, "Halt, or I'll shoot." With one eye on the passenger suspect's gun and one eye on the driver, who was now beginning to run to my left, away from his car, I cocked my revolver and leveled it at the driver fully meaning to shoot.

Like a bolt of lightning it hit me. If I missed the suspects, and I probably would because about seventy-five percent of the shots fired by police officers in gun battle miss the suspects, I stood a good chance of hitting an innocent person parked on the freeway.

I had already gotten a momentary glimpse of the horror-stricken faces of several of the people in the background. They looked so helpless, shocked, as though they were having a bad dream. Traffic was stopped. They were frozen. They couldn't help, only helplessly gape. For these motorists, the scene was like a bird's-eye view of the shootout at the "OK Corral."

My gut said, "A tenth of a second and a tenth of an inch of trigger pull and it would all be over." For some reason, somehow, I began to chase the suspect and tackled him about a car's length to the left of his opened door. At the same time, I kept one eye on the gun in the hands of the other suspect still in the car.

Within a few seconds, the driver suspect was subdued and was surprisingly submissive. I quickly dragged him back to the police car as the first backup unit responding to my "Officer Needs Help" call arrived.

I yelled, "Cuff him." Then I ran back to the Chevy where the passenger suspect was still seated and homing in with his revolver on every move I made.

I truly thought, "Bradley Maurice Phillips, your luck has run out now." However, those faces of innocent people in the background emerged again, yet my instinct still said, "Shoot or be shot!"

There was no turning back now. This was total commitment. That tenth-of-a-second, tenth-of-an-inch trigger pull decision still plagued me.

This time I yelled, "Drop the gun or I'll blow your head off." I knew this was not what was taught by the LAPD at the Police Academy, but they were carefully selected words. They were words from the bottom of my heart, and I certainly meant each word I uttered. I repeated it a second time, but with even more emotion.

Life and death were obviously less than a click away for both of us. He knew it. I knew it.

The suspect's gun twitched and quivered and finally dropped onto the floorboard. "Thank God!" I muttered under my breath, then crawled into the driver's seat facing the suspect. My right hand and revolver were shaking like a leaf in a heavy wind, but I quickly steadied my right hand by pointing my gun into the suspect's left ear, as I opened the passenger's door with my left hand and pushed him to the pavement, face down.

For the first time, I realized that my revolver had been cocked to double action with the hammer back since I had jumped out of the police vehicle upon stopping on the on-ramp. How did I manage to wrestle with both suspects and not pull the trigger less than that tenth of an inch?

The suspect's weapon was now safely tucked away in my belt, as I sat on top of him. While the suspect lay face down on the pavement, with both hands behind his head waiting to be handcuffed, people stared in amazement.

I quickly regained my composure, concealing my true fear, which meant that I was regaining full control and credit for the successful capture of these two "villains of society."

Removing my revolver from the suspect's ear, I then pointed it at the ground, held onto the hammer with my left hand and lightly pulled the trigger. The hammer released gently, just as the Colt Firearm Company had designed it to do, and thank God, it didn't go off. Quickly, I holstered my revolver and aggressively cuffed the disarmed suspect, pulling him to his feet with strength and authority.

My successful capture of the suspects would certainly earn me an "A" for today at work, especially as I saw my sergeant running toward me to assist with the arrest.

I informed the sergeant that he could Code 4 the location, which meant that no further assistance was needed. The situation was under control.

The sergeant took my prisoner in order to allow me to complete my investigation. I requested that he and the officer holding the driver to advise the suspects of their constitutional rights and transport them to the Parker Center for booking.

I looked to see if these glaring citizens were cheering me on. While I congratulated myself for the second or third time, the officer who was holding the driver of the Chevy walked up to me and tapped me on the shoulder.

He said, "Phillips, that first suspect, the driver…"

I interrupted, "Let's just advise them of their rights and transport them to Parker Center, ok?"

Again, he said, "Phillips," and I thought to myself, what does this guy want? I have handled everything by myself up to this point. Can't he simply advise the suspect of his Miranda rights and transport him? I'll even do the paperwork.

The officer, of Latin descent, again placed his hand on my shoulder and in a gesture of brotherly love said, without letting me interrupt again, "Phillips, the first suspect is not really a suspect. He was working in the parking lot on the northwest corner of 14th and Olive and was moving that white Chevy. The suspect came running up to the passenger's window, banged on the glass, and threatened the parking lot attendant. The suspect stuck his revolver to the driver's head and made him drive. This is when your pursuit began."

This information was like stripping a soldier of his Purple Heart. I blurted out, "No, why didn't he stop when I yelled at him?"

The officer continued, "The driver doesn't speak English. You see, he just came here from Mexico. He could not understand you, and he could not tell you that he had been kidnapped at gunpoint. He was running for his life."

I stood frozen and speechless for a few seconds. The slim, five-foot-six-inch, Hispanic kidnapped victim humbled me as I turned to face him. He lowered his chin and softly said, "Gracias, gracias." He did not realize that I had come closer to taking his life than that of the suspect's. Maybe it was best that he didn't know.

I slowly stepped closer, eyeballed him and then gently bounced my right fist off his left biceps and smiled. He beamed back at me with a sigh of relief. Although we spoke different languages, both of us had now communicated.

We called the tow service for the suspect's vehicle and tried to clear up the on-ramp havoc. About this time, the captain rolled up to the scene and, after a brief explanation by my sergeant, the captain walked over and shook my hand. He commended me for controlling this critical situation without firing a shot. I smiled and beamed, but inside I knew without a doubt, I certainly had *not* been in control of this episode.

Why in the world had I not shot the kidnapped driver? Why had my revolver not accidentally gone off while cocked, after chasing and wrestling the driver suspect? Why had my revolver not accidentally discharged when I crawled into the front seat and made contact with the passenger suspect who was definitely armed? Why didn't the passenger suspect shoot me? I thought, surely I was not in control.

Completing the Vehicle Impound Report for the tow truck operator, I muttered to myself, "Why was I so lucky?" Often I forget where my strength comes from.

On the way to my locker to change out of my uniform, I again contemplated the day's events. The suspect had just been paroled from San Quentin State Prison five days prior to this event. He wanted the gun to kill an informant who had helped send him to prison for four years earlier for first-degree burglary.

As you can imagine, I was late for school that evening, but I had gained an education that most people would never want to receive, much less have the opportunity to receive. The paperwork wasn't all that bad, either.

I thought to myself, the decisions an officer must make within the most critical tenth of a second boggle the mind. What if he makes the wrong choice? The Supreme Court can take ten months or two years to make their decision, and even then they often come up with a five-to-four split vote. Police officers need lots of help. They may think they are in control, but often they are not.

2

TAKE THE RIGHT TURN

It was still dark and cold at 5:55 a.m. as I parked my red VW bug about six blocks from the station. I picked up my.38 caliber revolver off the front seat and stuck it in my belt and slung my freshly cleaned uniform over my shoulder. I began the long hike to Parker Center and thought how unfair it was that most officers working at Central Division had no city parking provided as was done at all other LAPD divisions. It just wasn't fair.

I chuckled to myself as I remembered that I had enjoyed the walk before, and never complained about it until I heard Harold Hanks, a salty nineteen-year veteran, griping last week in roll call. Sergeant Adams had explained that city parking was based on seniority, which meant not only length of service but also rank. Hanks had the length of service but not the rank; however, he liked being a gruff street cop and really liked to complain.

Parker Center, which served as police headquarters and the home for the old Central Division, was packed with brass. As you would expect, R.H.I.P., Rank Had Its Privileges, and they got the convenient parking spaces.

Sergeant Adams had gone on to explain that someday a new Central facility would be built with adequate city parking for street cops, but Hanks just laughed it off. I wondered if the sergeant was just joking with us.

By now I was halfway to the building. It was early as roll call didn't start until 7:15 a.m. However, I took a lot of pride in polishing my badge, buttons and leather gear. I'd been off for two days and was anxious to get back to work. By arriving early I'd have plenty of time to go up to the police cafeteria, on the eighth floor, for breakfast and conversation with the other day watch officers. The brass wouldn't take over the cafeteria until 9:00 a.m. Then it was "their cafeteria," or at least that's what Hanks had said.

Being a twenty-two-year-old bachelor, I found myself eating out most of the time.

Six days had elapsed since the excitement on the Harbor Freeway. Things had been routine prior to my taking two days off. Just one minor felony arrest, a couple of drunks, a few minor police reports, but a relatively large number of neighbor and family disputes. That bugged me. Why couldn't adults get along? Their disputes seemed so childish from a police officer's standpoint.

After roll call, I checked out a shotgun, five shells, a spotlight, flares and all the other police equipment that makes an officer feel he needs a wheelbarrow to carry it to the police car in one trip.

I left Parker Center and after going two blocks, realized I'd better return for gasoline as the night and morning watch had again failed to gas the vehicle before checking it in at the end of watch. Although it was Thursday, it seemed like Monday to me because I'd been off a couple of days. I was also a little slow getting started. The morning seemed to drag. It was now nearly 11:00 a.m. With the temperature already in the high 80s, it was getting to be a hot, stuffy, smoggy day. The radio had been slow so I had run about six vehicles for "wants," but had come up with no "hits."

I needed a "line for the log" so I cruised to the top of the hill near Silver Lake Boulevard and Burbank Boulevard and glanced at the steep steps of the large gray house which was the home of Chief Clayton T. Smith. 1L1 could always get a line by logging this as a "security check." C.S. Hardy, an eighteen-year veteran, had taught me this.

As I descended the hill and rounded the curve on Edgewater Terrace and approached Silver Lake Boulevard I debated whether to go to the right so I could cruise by the reservoir or go left and head toward Tommy's for a greasy chiliburger. The reservoir sounded better so I took a right.

While completing the right turn, my mind flashed back several months to the night I had worked the drunk wagon with Vasquez. I had been driving north on San Pedro Street and stopped at the red light at 5th Street. We had nine drunks in the back of the vehicle. As we made a left turn and went westbound up the hill we heard the rear door banging open. We immediately stopped and ran back to see the drunks rolling down the hill. Vasquez and I scooped up all we could find and, thank God, none were seriously injured. Quickly, we got them back inside the wagon and counted noses. One was missing.

11

We hustled back to the beat officers who had made the arrest and ripped up copies of the Short Form Arrest Report.

That turn had been a "wrong" turn, but if we could have caught that pedestrian rascal who had walked behind the wagon and opened up the rear door it would have been a "right" turn. Boy, was that embarrassing, but lucky for us, the sergeant did not find out about it.

A short block later my mind was back on the reservoir. A northbound light-blue '64 Ford made a left turn in front of me onto Armstrong Street. Their turn was not unsafe, or unusual, but something about the two male occupants inside struck me as unusual.

Neither suspect appeared to eyeball me and that was strange. My gut gave me a quick jab. Why were they going out of their way not to eyeball me? They had to have seen the black and white with "lights" on top. There were no other vehicles around and I was directly in front of them.

As they completed their turn in front of me, I made a right turn and followed them onto Armstrong Street. I picked up the mike then hesitated for a moment. If I ran another "want" on a vehicle, which at that time required a lengthy hand search, and came up with another "no hit" today, my sergeant might justifiably criticize me and say, "Phillips, don't you ever do anything except run vehicle wants, and check the chief's house?" I guess my guilt of looking for a line on the log was showing through.

I had been trained in observation and my instinct said run it. With the mike in my right hand near the lower portion of the steering wheel, so as not to tip off the two suspects, I keyed it and with my lips barely moving said, "1L1 requesting a rolling want on Queen, Edward, Mary, Four, Five, One."

I appeared to be unconcerned with the suspects as I glanced to my left at the reservoir, which seemed to be so peaceful as we cruised through the clean residential area.

Time always seemed longer when you were waiting for something, especially as I had run a "rolling want," which had priority over routine vehicle checks.

The suspects made a left into Chadwick Avenue and I casually followed. At Hyperion they caught the red light and stopped in the left lane. Still trying not to look too obvious, I pulled to a stop behind them and kept rubbernecking to the right and left, hoping to give the impression that I was not following them but merely traveling the same route. The thing that really kept giving me butterflies in my stomach was that, out of the corner of my eye, I could tell that both suspects were still quite stiff-necked. Were they role playing as I was?

My gut took a double jab when I saw that they were not going straight as I anticipated. The light was now green and for the first time I noticed their left turn directional light was flashing. Had the driver just decided to turn left to lose me when they saw that my directional was not on for a left turn?

I muttered to myself, "They know good and well that I'm behind them. I know they do. Those stiff-necked turkeys must be hot or I am overreacting because I have been off work for two days and am itching for a hit?"

"Come on, come on, Communications. Is the car stolen?" I breathed.

They completed the turn with me on their tail. It seemed as though ten minutes had elapsed since I had run the license number and still their eyes were glued straight ahead. This would never hold up in court as probable cause to stop them. I could see the judge literally throwing me out of court. What I really needed was a "hit."

As we stopped for a red light at Hyperion and Park Boulevard, my stomach was churning, just as it had on the Harbor Freeway several days earlier. My mind was racing a mile a minute. These guys had to be superhot. I just knew it or, again, was I overreacting? My street sense had been wrong before, however, not very often. They could be robbery suspects not just simple car thieves. I felt that if I had to handle both of them by myself they were going to blow me out of my boots. Choosing to get the greasy chiliburger didn't seem so bad now.

When the light turned green they continued southbound and I turned right. As the '64 Ford got out of sight, a half block south, I made a quick U-turn then another right turn to again head south on Hyperion.

I figured if these guys were hot and I turned off and then came charging up behind them, they would "rabbit." It was worth a try. I pressed the gas pedal to the floor and charged up behind the suspects as though I knew something but they didn't flinch.

At this point I had almost forgotten that I was waiting for the results of my rolling want. Let down, depressed, feeling a little psycho and paranoid, I was nearly ready to make another U-turn and head for Tommy's when Control 1 chattered. "1L1, Queen, Edward, Mary, Four, Five, One is a Venice stolen, DR #1928-497-725."

I perked up quickly and grabbed the mike in my right hand. "Cool it! Cool it!" I kept muttering to myself. They'll realize I made them if I don't play it right.

In a low tone of voice I keyed the mike and said, "1L1, that was a rolling want. I am southbound on Hyperion just passing Palm Crest Drive following the suspects who are in a two-door blue Ford."

The link operator took over the frequency from the regularly assigned radio-telephone operator and in his distinct voice announced, "All units, all frequencies standby, 1L1 is following a stolen vehicle southbound on Hyperion just passing Palm Crest Drive. 1L1, come in."

All field officers love this. This told every police officer in the city of Los Angeles that 1L1 was center stage. Then, I thought: Six days ago I nearly blew it. Am I going to do it again? I think I have over committed myself again. Help! Help!

I responded, "1L1, the vehicle is still southbound on Hyperion with two robbery suspects, both twenty-five to thirty years, male, Caucasian, both wearing khaki shirts. Officer needs help." I wanted to include in the description that they both had very stiff necks but I didn't.

Control 1 came back in and repeated the message to the officers on duty as I convinced myself that I had five more hours before EOW and was going to be in no hurry with this caper. Besides, there would be lots of paperwork to fill out on this one. I followed patiently, still pretending to sightsee to my right and left, realizing that they had nearly circled around Silver Lake. Now they knew without a doubt, I was following them; however, my best bet was to buy time.

We continued on Hyperion for another mile, which seemed to take twenty-five to thirty minutes. The radio continued to repeat my location as I informed Control 1. At Fountain we again stopped for the red light.

To my surprise the radio announced, "6W3 has the vehicles in sight and will help 1L1 pull the vehicle over at Hyperion and

14

Fountain." My stomach churned. Not in my entire life had I had trouble in spotting an unmarked detective car. The four-door, cheaply equipped, Chevrolet with black wall tires, drab, faded colors and twin antennas was always as obvious as the black and whites with cherries on top. Everyone could spot them, but where was this detective unit?

Then I breathed as I spotted him near the northeast corner. The detective eyeballed me as the light turned green for Hyperion traffic. I flipped on my reds and beeped the horn as the detective blew his red light to pull up alongside the suspects on their left. He pointed his revolver at the driver.

At this point, the driver accelerated powerfully ahead and swerved to his left forcing the detective into the southbound lane, barely missing another car head on. The race was on!

As I glanced in my mirror, I could see 6W3 joining the pursuit about 100 yards behind. As funny as it may seem, I could not get it out of my mind how much difficulty I had in broadcasting in the pursuit six days earlier. Maybe I could perfect the technique for the department.

The next five minutes were spent weaving in and around the residential neighborhood northwest of Sunset and Fountain. I was obviously somewhere in Hollywood Division as I didn't recognize the street names and was completely lost. I wasn't even sure in what direction I was traveling.

Two more blocks and the suspects made a quick right. Their plan almost worked as they nearly lost me on this turn. I skidded around the corner and just missed an elderly lady who was scrambling to get back to the curb.

When I glanced in my rear view mirror, I could see the street lit up like Christmas. There had to be at least ten black and whites with their red lights on, following me up the incline.

Control 1 came in and said, "1L1, give your location."

I keyed the mike and in a bewildered tone of voice, said, "1L1, I don't know where I am. Have the units following 1L1 give my location. I'm lost!"

The link operator had to know by now that I was a lost rookie. He paused, then announced, "Any unit following 1L1 come in and give his location. He's lost."

A two-officer Hollywood unit, 6A52, responded that we were now northbound on Pascual Avenue heading for Griffith Park.

I had been to Griffith Park only twice prior to this pursuit and on both occasions had gotten disoriented.

As we wound around the hills near the golf course, the suspects nearly missed the left curve where the golf course sprinklers had gotten the street wet and slippery.

Again, I convinced myself I was not going to be over aggressive in this pursuit. There were still several hours prior to EOW and there was no school tonight. I had plenty of time.

I tried holding the microphone in my right hand, left hand, between my legs and over the sun visor. Officer John Starr had been right, I conceded, when he taught our Communication Procedures class at the Police Academy. There is no easy way for a one-officer unit to drive in a pursuit and broadcast at the same time.

One strange thing kept haunting me. As the suspects rounded the curves to the left, I could see the driver clearly through his open window. The driver kept biting on his fingers, not on his nails. He appeared to be biting on the underneath side. Strange, but I'd seen crazier things occurring out on the streets.

6A52 then advised Control 1 that we were approaching the observatory, which was news to me. I felt more secure knowing that at least someone knew where we were headed. As we rounded the top of the hill, I saw the dome of the very large observatory on the skyline. The parking lot was packed with school kids and several school buses. This obviously was not the ideal setting for a pursuit or a gun battle.

A bus driver swerved to miss the suspect's car head-on. The driver of the '64 Ford whipped a quick "U" then started back down the hill with 1L1 on his tail. As I glanced in my rear-view mirror, I noticed the bus whose driver had swerved to miss the suspect, was now blocking the roadway down the hill after apparently stalling. I also saw that 6W3, 6A52 and the other units were blocked by the stalled school bus. My heart pounded and now I again felt as if I was running naked, lost in a jungle.

Suddenly, as we traveled along the winding road in the heavily wooded area, we came to a fork in the road with no street sign posted. The Ford driver took the right turn and I followed.

16

I had experienced safety and security the past ten minutes with the other units only a glimpse away in my rear-view mirror. Now they were out of sight and all the units would miss the right turn if the first unit following me missed it. With 6W3 having been in sight and knowing exactly where I was, the need for help didn't seem so important. But now, I thought, this is a potentially dangerous situation by myself. It hit me. Use what you have. I keyed the mike and yelled, "Tell all the units following 1L1 to take a right turn at the fork in the road."

The radio was silent. Then the link operator said, "1L1, give your location."

I panicked again and admitted, "I'm lost, but tell all units following 1L1 to take a right turn at the fork in the road."

The veteran link operator must have thought this phrase was out of some western movie then finally, in a questioning tone of voice, said, "All units following 1L1, take a right turn at the fork in the road." Without his broadcast on the old police radio, none of the units would hear my location or directions.

I knew everyone in Communications Division had to be laughing about this descriptive pursuit, but I was lost and about at my wit's end.

As we descended the winding hill, how I hoped that at least one unit made the right turn. Suddenly, I saw the suspects negotiate the left turn curve too fast and brake sharply to avoid colliding with the trees and embankment on the right side of the road. Their car must have stalled as the driver looked panicked and jumped out. I jammed on the brakes and swerved to the right. I threw the car into Park and exited in a crouched position with my revolver drawn.

The driver faced me as he jumped out of his car. He crouched and leveled his revolver as he aimed it at me. Suddenly, out of nowhere, 6W3 came roaring down the hill, skidded and swerved so as to miss me and my police cruiser. He barely missed me, but rammed the rear of the suspect's vehicle. The suspect's car immediately caught fire and was quickly engulfed in flames. The driver was so confused by the crash he turned without shooting and began running toward the thickly wooded area. Instinctively, I ran to the right side of the burning car and pulled the other suspect through the passenger's window. Momentarily I thought maybe I should have let him fry, but

I quickly cuffed him as he coughed and moaned from a head injury, smoke inhalation and burns he had received on his arms, legs and upper body. After pushing the suspect to the ground, I reached back into the burning car and grabbed the suspect's pistol off the front seat. The metal on the pistol was hot and I singed the hair on the top of my left hand and arm, left side of my head and eyebrows from the flames.

As the stunned detective approached me, I yelled, "Take the cuffed suspect." I ran into the woods where I had seen the driver go. He had a good thirty-second lead on me, but he had to be as confused as I was. The collision and the car now being engulfed in flames, were totally unexpected.

I quickly pursued him and yelled, "Police officer, put your hands up!" What a bluff. I couldn't see the suspect. I guess I was hoping he would just stop, throw down his gun, put his hands up and wait for me to take him into custody. This was not a reflection of my training, but rather a creative impulse from my brain.

Apparently, 6A52 had skidded to a stop behind my car. My peripheral vision provided me a glance of the passenger officer coming to help me after the detective pointed in my direction. As I ran into the woods I felt so vulnerable. The suspect could probably see me yet I didn't know where he was. My adrenaline was certainly flowing.

I remembered what another officer once told me about his calling for help in a prior shooting situation in a downtown alley. He said he yelled and yelled for help but no one heard him until he blew his whistle. He took out his fifty-cent plastic whistle, blew it with all his might and got help. But, today, it probably wouldn't work in the woods. I ran down the path about seventy-five yards where the path stopped, but did not catch a glimpse of the suspect.

Finally, I stopped and listened carefully but I couldn't hear anything. I waited a few seconds then saw the uniformed officer from 6A52 about thirty feet away, approaching me. Then, *boom-boom*, out of the bushes about five feet from me, I saw two flashes. It was all happening in slow motion. At the same time, I felt as if someone had taken a full swing with an ax and sliced into my left foot. The pain was unbelievably sharp. Then I felt as if someone had stuck a hot, pointed branding iron through my right side. I felt it start just above my belt line slightly on the right side just below my vest and go all the way through my body exiting out my back. My flesh felt as if it was burning in both areas. The two bullets hurt intensely.

I dropped both my gun and the one I had grabbed out of the burning car. The pain was excruciating and the capture of the suspect was now out of my mind. My own physical needs overrode any goals and objectives of the LAPD.

The other officer must have seen me fall to the ground. He fired nine shots into the bushes and quickly stuck a new clip of ammo into his automatic. Things were still seeming to happen in slow motion, but before I passed out, the suspect fell through the bushes with blood everywhere. The last thing I remember was the suspect getting an LAPD boot kicked into his limp head and another officer holding my bloody hand and telling me an ambulance was en route to the scene.

I didn't remember the ambulance ride or arriving at Central Receiving Hospital. After seven hours in the operating room and five hours in the recovery room, the anesthetic began wearing off. My body didn't handle drugs well. My mind wandered in and out of various dreams. Many involved various police situations. All were strange indeed.

When I regained full consciousness, my mother and father were seated in my room next to the bed. My mother said I was going to be okay, but that I had been shot. My father explained that I had been shot twice. One shot had hit my left foot and the other my right side. They both told me the doctors had assured them I would fully recover. After further inquiry by me, they said the doctor expected me to heal, totally regain my health and be able to return to police work. On the latter point, my mother disagreed with the doctor.

Apparently, Sergeant Adams had been waiting outside my room since I had been moved from the recovery room. My mother said he wanted to see me. She invited him in and, to my surprise, he didn't address me as "Phillips."

He said, "Bradley, we are glad you are going to be okay. Chief Smith was here earlier and asked me to convey his sincere hope for your speedy recovery."

Funny I thought, but it took two bullets to get Adams to call me Bradley. It was good to see someone in blue, specifically LAPD blue!

3

MEET THE TEACHER

Seven months passed before I could put the blue uniform on again and return to work. The watch commander assigned me to station duties such as the desk officer position or station security for another three months. These were nothing jobs, but they helped me pass the time before I could obtain a full return to duty that would allow me to go back to the streets.

I worked diligently with the physical therapist three times a week to speed my recovery. I also pushed myself at home to ensure my recovery time was as fast as humanly possible. Never would I admit the real pain I still had: the fear of the chief's retiring me from the job due to my injuries.

The passenger suspect from my shooting caper in Griffith Park copped out to grand theft auto, twelve bank robberies and assault with a deadly weapon on a police officer. He also acknowledged they were en route to rob another bank when I started my pursuit.

I thought it was interesting that both suspects had their fingers taped with Scotch tape. That was what I had seen the driver biting to try to get off his fingers while I was chasing them. Anyway, the incident would send him back to San Quentin for a third time. However, with time off for good behavior, he would be back on the streets in less than ten years.

There was talk among the politicians of creating a "3-strikes" law so that people such as these would not be able to continue getting out of prison and repeating the offense. Three chances were more than any criminal deserved!

I didn't like that the district attorney was not trying him for attempted murder on a police officer, but this was the criminal justice system. The plea bargaining ensured the district attorney of credit for a conviction without the expense of a lengthy trial with the possibility, not probability, of the slime ball beating the rap.

Because the other suspect was dead at the scene, the taxpayers had no additional expense associated with exercising his judicial rights. He had spent eighteen of his thirty-nine years on earth behind bars.

February was a good month for me. I returned to full duty and was back in a black and white. That felt great!

Sergeant Adams presented me an Award of Merit for the shooting caper, but there was no recommendation for the Medal of Valor. I guess they didn't think I should have gone in the woods without more backup. Or, maybe it was because they didn't like my broadcasting of my location during the long pursuit, or maybe, because I didn't blow my fifty-cent plastic whistle when chasing after the suspect in the woods. Oh well, it didn't matter. I was alive and well and back on the streets.

When Sergeant Adams gave me the award, all the guys razzed me when he read it at roll call. But we all, especially cops, crave recognition for a job well done.

The rear row of the roll-call room was still reserved for the "old salts" of the watch. They would grumble under their breath and occasionally become loud and boisterous while challenging the system, but these two or three guys always controlled themselves just enough to prevent a charge of insubordination, an unsatisfactory rating report or "freeway therapy."

Freeway therapy meant, for example, if you lived in San Pedro and were assigned to Harbor Division you could be transferred to Foothill Division some sixty-two miles away. If these three things were not enough to restrain them, there was always the "wheel" where they could be rotated to a different watch each month.

This has a yo-yo effect on the entire body system and social life. These actions were seldom, if ever, used as we were well aware that management had this as an option. The mere threat of this possibility helped to make police associations, which are actually police unions, quite strong.

The old-timers would test new sergeants to find out if they were leaders or followers. If they were leaders, no problem; but if they were followers, they were led down the primrose path!

Along with most of the officers on the watch, I sat in the middle of the roll-call room between the third and fifth rows. By far, the majority of the officers were professionals who chose the LAPD as a career not just a job. The selection and training process was proof of this fact. Responsibility, honor and action had been shown by surveys to be the leading factors in attracting officers to the LAPD.

21

Lieutenant Mark Allen was the day watch commander and he had the respect of every officer on the watch. He was positive in his leadership techniques and inspired high morale and productivity from the troops.

Allen set a good example for the troops. Later he would become a commander then leave the LAPD to become chief of a small police department in Northern California. After Allen was double-dipping on the two police retirements, the governor would appoint him as a judge in the superior court near San Francisco which would eventually net him a triple-dipper status in the pensions.

With this many pensions, all he'd have to do is live to be 100 and he'd get to milk the system to the end. As a young cop, I could not grasp the magnitude of three pensions. Could anyone beat that?

The day was Tuesday, February 23, following the long Washington's birthday holiday weekend. This meant most of the crimes which had occurred over the three-day weekend would probably be discovered and reported between 6:00 a.m. and 10:00 a.m. The lieutenant completed roll call rapidly and said, "Let's get a cup of coffee and hit the streets a little early!"

After showing 1L1 clear, I made sure my assigned car had gasoline, then left the station and headed west on First Street to Couger's Donut Shop at Park Avenue and Alvarado. After two donuts and half a cup of coffee, my radio chattered with, "1L1, meet the teacher - Burglary Investigation - Lawrence Street Elementary School, 3500 Monterey Street."

I "rogered" the call and poured the balance of the hot colored water out in the trash. I thought to myself, better there than in my stomach. As usual, it was too strong and didn't taste good.

As I headed north on Alvarado it seemed strange that Lawrence Street School would be on Monterey Street. Why didn't they name it Monterey Street Elementary School? Oh well!

As I turned right onto Monterey, I experienced recollections of the Police Academy, which was just on the other side of the hill. I especially remembered working so hard and long to prepare for the academy, particularly by jogging.

Officer Gary Mitchem, our physical fitness instructor, insisting on jogging our guts out, but I was smaller than he was and thought my endurance was good, if not better, than his. I jogged at the head of the class. When Mitchem was leading the class, I would go out of my way to control my breathing and sight-see during the scenic jog through Elysian Park.

This drove Mitchem out of his mind as he would increase the pace trying to make me hurt. I would increase my pace to a little faster than his and he would use his deep command voice and say, "Ok Phillips - hold it down!" I slowed and chuckled inside as I was glad Mitchem didn't call my bluff. It was like psychological warfare. I really did hurt inside, but I successfully concealed it.

There it was, 3500 Monterey Street, Lawrence Street Elementary School. I was still puzzled by the name. Then I saw that the entrance to the main building, which was older, faced Lawrence Street. The puzzle was now solved.

As I walked down the hallway in the newer and larger building toward the office, I saw two boys spot me and dart into the principal's office to tip him off that a cop was present. The principal immediately met me at the doorway and escorted me to another building. We checked out the cafeteria and several classrooms on the first floor. Then we went upstairs to the northeast corner classroom where the burglary had occurred.

Kids had apparently broken in over the weekend via a fire escape, and had taken an expensive record player and cassette player which were personal property of the teacher.

With all reports completed, I was now ready to return to the streets. As I walked down the stairs, I noticed the other teachers had apparently finished their morning coffee. They were leaving the teacher's cafeteria, en masse, to get ready for the arrival of their students.

A young, good-looking teacher caught my eye. I slowed my pace to match hers so as to arrive at the foot of the stairs at the same time. As we met I smiled and being on my best behavior, asked, "Was anything taken from your room?" I knew she wouldn't know, as she surely had been off for the three-day weekend and was probably not as anxious as the elderly teacher to check out her room before a morning cup of coffee with the other, more sociable teachers.

Naturally, she inquired as to what had happened and, of course, I blew it all out of proportion with an exaggerated crime story. I then suggested we check out her classroom as though the culprits might still be there!

After ten more minutes of small talk in her room, she pointed out two burnt matches and noted that several felt-tip pens appeared to be missing from her desk. Great! Now I would have to get her name and other pertinent information; that is, for the police report, of course. Never did I dream that this teacher, Marie, would be my bride in a year!

After taking the report to the station, old Sergeant Evons, who had a three-digit serial number and hash marks up to his sergeant stripes, bowed his head, peeped through his bifocals and scrutinized the burglary report. He grumbled under his breath about how the new rookies didn't have the writing skills that more senior officers had. This actually meant that the sergeant liked me because he didn't rip it up and tell me to start all over again!

After making me change three words and add a couple of commas, he signed the report and pointed to the door, meaning *Hit the streets again.* I obeyed without question or comment.

Two days later a senior officer with two years on the job bumped me off 1L1. This proved that time-in-grade was worth something. Sergeant Evons fiddled with the assignment board and put me on 1U2, an unmarked report car, because Higgins, a twenty-three year police officer, was off sick.

Most street cops hated this assignment as they were given report calls all day. This meant lots of paperwork, and little, if any, real action. I was determined to turn 1U2 into a something job if I was going to work it for eight hours.

Higgins was content with the assignment and Sergeant Evons always let him work 1U2 in plain clothes. The public thought Higgins was a big-time detective. All he needed was a hat and he could fit right into the "Hat Squad" on the third floor of Parker Center, in Robbery Division.

Sergeant Evons, who was the acting watch commander today, completed roll call and said, "Go do it!"

I walked up to the raised platform and supervisors' table and said, "Sarge, how about letting me go out in plain clothes today like Higgins does in 1U2?"

Evons grinned and replied, "Whoever heard of a rookie working as a detective?"

I turned red and beamed, "Come on, Sarge, it will be a good experience for me. You are going to make something of me yet, aren't you?"

This made it easier for the sergeant. Now his decision of "yes" or "no" seemed more important, at least to him. He wrinkled his mouth and replied, "Okay! Okay! But hurry up and get out of your uniform."

I went to my locker and was glad I had left an older sports coat and slacks, white shirt and tie there for the unexpected call to court, special police assignment or unexpected last-minute date.

Phil, the vehicle dispatcher, grinned when I handed him a vehicle authorization card for an unmarked car. After ten years' experience he knew this was a big deal for a young rookie. With a full tank of gas in the car, a half cup of coffee and two Cougar's donuts, I again headed for Lawrence Street Elementary School, just in case a follow-up investigation was necessary or required!

Well, lo and behold, there she was, the cute teacher. Marie didn't see me as I cruised by, but I spotted her as she walked toward the newer building. What luck, I thought.

Then, up and over the hill I drove to the academy for weapons qualification. My timing was perfect. I'd be in an unmarked detective car and in a suit. Obviously, my peers would think I'd made the big time in only sixteen months after graduating from the academy. It was impossible, but it would be a challenge to pull off.

After shooting 283 out of 300 I went inside the warm restaurant that was like a private club. I didn't see but three people I recognized and they obviously didn't even know me. What a flop the trip had been, however, I did get my February qualification out of the way. This always seemed to be such a waste of time to the troops but not for those responsible for the city's liability.

As I started the car, I glanced over at the eighth-of-a-mile track, which again brought back memories of academy days. These were good memories that I knew I would have for the rest of my life, but today I hoped some day the pain from the gunshots would go away completely and I would be back to my full physical strength.

The three months of physical training at the academy included a lot of stress, but I had experienced this in basic training in the Army and also while attending OCS, Officers Candidate School. The Police Academy stress was different. This was not just a temporary thing for me.

By the time I made it to the academy, police work was to be my lifetime career, my chosen profession. I was motivated and my struggles to become a police officer had really prepared me and matured my attitude.

The P.T., physical training, seemed to be the hardest for everyone, but I had spent two months preparing physically for this grind, so it came easily for me. Most of the recruits were physically beat by the time they got home at night so they didn't feel like studying. I felt great as I was in good shape, so I would study, thus making the academics easy.

Firearm training was another important area. If a cop had reasonable coordination, the excellent firearm instructors could teach them this skill without difficulty.

As I cleared from the qualification visit to the academy, I concluded that physical training and attitude were the key factors for success at the Police Academy. The next six hours involved nine crime reports taken and a zero on my recap sheet, where it counted! I couldn't figure out how Higgins could do this for twenty-three years, but he liked it.

Now I was again only two blocks from the school. I decided it was worth a try. I cruised eastbound on Monterey and spotted her again. What luck, twice in one day! Her class was out on the playground. I pulled to the curb and stopped by the gate. The kids waved and obviously knew I was a cop, but the teacher was looking in the other direction trying to referee a kickball game. I motioned to the kids to tell her to come over to the car. She turned and, with a questionable look, stared at me as though I was a suspicious person.

Finally, one of the fifth-grade boys clued her in that I was the "man," as I motioned for her to come to the fence. Hesitantly, the cautious teacher walked toward the gate, keeping one eye on her class and the other eye questioning who was calling her over to the fence. She finally recognized me and said, "Oh, hi! I didn't know you were also a detective."

I stuttered, and replied, "Oh, uh!" then paused, avoided a direct answer, and continued. "I was wondering if you found anything else missing at the school. Just doing a little follow-up work." This was followed by ten minutes of small talk, as she continued to keep an eye on her class and occasionally responded to one of the student's questions or complaints.

She was being very cautious and taking things one step at a time.

Finally, after a lot of slick maneuvering, I extended a casual invitation to go for a cup of coffee after work some day. She grinned and after carefully clarifying the exact rendezvous circumstances, consented to a quick cup of coffee at four o'clock the next afternoon. Friday would work out for both of us. Great, and away I sped. Now I was really motivated to do some serious police work.

The next day I was back in uniform working 1L1, filling in for the slightly senior officer that was on a day off. Today's schedule was going to be tight. If I were to meet the teacher at four, I would have to get the sergeant to let me go EOW about three o'clock. Which sergeant would be my best bet?

Sergeant Montgomery was still on probation, so he might be uncooperative. Sergeant Adams was too straight-arrow. It boiled down to Evons. It was he or no one. So I returned to Parker Center and marched into the watch commander's office.

Evons looked up from a map sprawled over his desk and, not in his usual manner, said, "What do you think?" Should I take the northern route or the southern route? I think I'll go north!" I wondered, what in the world is he talking about, and glanced down to see the map was of the United States.

I blurted out, "No Sarge, take the southern route, always!"

He retorted, "Why?"

"This time of the year there is more snow on the roads in the North and the southern route is more scenic," I answered.

Evons again wrinkled his mouth and said, "Yeah, I think you are right," as he glanced back at the map.

Then I slipped it in. "Sarge, I need to take Code 7 just prior to end of watch, okay?"

Without thinking, looking up or getting his thoughts off his map, he muttered, "Okay, okay."

I quickly did an about-face and headed for the street. As I left the station I had to chuckle when a thought hit me. The sergeant must have been plotting his trip to Texas, where he was planning to retire. I had heard him talking about this as long as I had been assigned to Central Division.

The funny thing was that I had "shot from the hip." I had a fifty-fifty chance of being right. Should I take the northern route or southern route? Maybe this put the sergeant in the right frame of mind to bend the rule on my Code 7 request.

All the sergeants had been police officers and they knew that Code 7 just prior to EOW was a way to get off work forty-five minutes early. Besides, my training officers had taught me that a police officer should never go without a full stomach, even if it was a quick, greasy chiliburger while on the run to the next radio call.

Things looked really promising as I left Parker Center, then the radio interrupted with, "1L1, possible DB, ambulance en route, 7927 Rio Park Avenue, Apartment 206. 1L1, handle your call Code 2." As I "rogered" the call the inside of my mouth got real dry. I did not like DB calls and hoped that I would never reach the point where I was so cold that the emotion of the loved ones didn't somehow touch me.

Maybe it would *not* be a dead body but just a very sick person. Then I recalled that I had never heard of anyone receiving a possible DB call without it being the real thing. The odds just weren't in my favor.

As I headed west on Sunset then north on Rio Park Avenue, I spotted a strange looking woman, probably in her eighties. She was dressed in an old faded robe, standing in front of an older apartment complex. This was obviously the location because she was on the west side of the street in the 7900 block. Clever, I thought, east is even and south is the same. (This was an easy way to distinguish on which side of the street house numbers were located in the City of Los Angeles.)

As I got closer, she began to wave frantically, fearing that I would pass the apartment building. There had to be a DB inside, I could read it on her face. I pulled to the wrong side of the street and flipped on the red and amber lights so the ambulance crew would easily spot the location when they approached.

I jumped out, grabbed my hat and put it on my head. The only advantage of the hat was to make me look older and pacify my sergeant, should he drive up.

The lady grabbed my right arm and pleaded: "Help, help me, please! It's my husband. He won't wake up. Please officer, you will help me, won't you?"

"Sure I will," I replied, putting my arm around her, trying to calm her down.

"Where is he?" I asked.

Her cracking voice squeaked, "Up the stairs on the left, the second door. Please hurry."

I pulled away and ran to the stairs, grabbing the metal rail and taking the steps two at a time. The door was open so I entered the dimly-lit room with older, drab-colored furniture. No one was in sight. I hurried through another door and there lying on the bed was an elderly man. He looked to be at least eighty. I froze in my tracks. With his skin a grayish white, he was obviously dead.

My mind flashed again. We all know death, like taxes, is inevitable. Why can't we just simply accept it?

The moment I stood there frozen seemed like thirty minutes, then I heard the siren of the approaching ambulance. I slowly walked over to the old man. He looked to be at peace. I couldn't help but think that some day I would also be dead. Is there really life after death? I wondered.

I noticed a Holy Bible on the bedside table. It looked worn and frayed, like the furniture and the old man.

By now the ambulance attendants from Central Receiving Hospital were rushing in. "In here," I said, as they entered the living room. As the first attendant entered the bedroom he slowed as he spotted the victim.

He paused, then said, "Dead about six hours, I would say."

How do you figure?" I stuttered.

"*Rigor mortis* begins to set in within four or five hours after actual death and it's complete in about eight to ten hours," he retorted.

"Yeah, I know," was my reply as I didn't want to appear like a stupid, inexperienced rookie or admit that I always got "*rigor mortis*" and "*post-mortem lividity*" mixed up.

"I really didn't help the lady much, did I?" I said under my breath, hoping no one heard me.

By this time the other attendant, the older of the two, spoke up and said, "Maybe you had better confirm her suspicions." I swallowed hard and hid the lump in my throat as I walked toward the front door.

I could see her at the foot of the stairs with her head in her hands, weeping. Slowly, I descended the stairs and walked close to her. The poor lady, who reminded me very much of my grandmother, looked up at me as I said, "I'm sorry." She embraced me as though I were her son and had kept my word by helping her husband.

It wasn't anything I had done. She just needed someone, anyone, to support and comfort her. She sobbed heavily and stated that he had suffered from heart trouble for the past twenty years and just last month his doctor had said he was doing well.

We walked back up to her apartment and I tried to comfort her and make her feel as well as possible under the circumstances. The other neighbors stood outside and watched as two other elderly ladies assisted me. The neighbors were all helpful and took over so I could go on with my necessary work.

The ambulance attendants covered the body with a white sheet, shut the bedroom door, handed me a DB slip and courteously exited after telling the new widow, "Sorry, ma'am."

The DB slip showed DOA at 8:42 a.m. and listed his age as eighty-six years, which they obtained from identification, driver's license, and one of the neighbors in the living room.

After ascertaining that the widow had a son living in the Eagle Rock area, I phoned his house. His wife took the message and assured me she would pick him up at work and be right over. This was a great relief.

I called DHD, Detective Headquarters Division, and they advised me it was a coroner's case because the victim had not been treated by a doctor within the last ten days. DHD was dispatching a couple of detectives and would notify the coroner.

During the half-hour before the son and daughter-in-law arrived, I tried to calm the widow and provide her some peace of mind. I walked back into the bedroom, picked up the worn Bible, thumbed through it and read her several verses. This seemed to be reassuring to her as she said, "Yes, God is in control. I know that I will join Carl again in heaven." Then she looked me directly in the eye and, as the tears vanished, said, "You see, we believe in Jesus Christ and He will never let us down."

I replied, "Yeah," and got a little misty-eyed myself as I thought how much easier some Christians seemed to accept death.

Another forty-five minutes and two plain-clothes detectives were in charge of the scene with the deputy coroner doing his thing. With the son and his wife now taking care of his mother, I departed, again showing 1L1 clear.

I fastened my seat belt, wiped the perspiration from my forehead and glanced in the mirror at myself. I muttered, "Phillips, this is one reason why police officers have a twenty year retirement system." The stress on an officer in these types of situations is difficult to measure. This experience hurt nearly as much as the bullet wounds in my body. Well, maybe not quite as much, but close. I didn't like these emotional and stressful situations.

Then I thought back to the widow as I drove north through the park, which seemed so peaceful. I concluded that the emotional drain in handling the dead-body call was as stressful as that in the shooting incident ten months earlier in Griffith Park, even though the latter resulted in much greater physical injuries to myself.

Three o'clock rolled around fast after one drunk arrest, one stolen-vehicle report and two neighbor-dispute calls, after squeezing in the chiliburger on company time. I debated, then decided not to take credit for the death report on my recap because the detectives handled the brief, one-page Death Report that in essence said, "the end," for Carl.

I fueled the car as I wished the night and morning watch would do, then headed for my locker. By 3:20 p.m. my log was complete and I was in civvies and ready to meet the teacher.

Hiking, at nearly a jog, back to my VW, I headed for Lawrence Street Elementary School. I was early and the kids were gone by now so I hopped up the stairs to Room 222. I slowed, composed myself for the encounter and in a controlled voice said, "Hi!" as I walked into her room.

After the routine of locking her classroom, walking to the office and checking in her keys, we headed for Durango's on Sunset

Boulevard just four blocks away. There was something special about Marie. At least she had me on cloud nine, but I was going to cool it.

We finished drinking several cups of coffee then returned to the car. It was now 4:40 p.m. and I couldn't believe it! The civilian parking checker had written me a parking citation - a parking ticket. Hertel's, the police tow service, was now backing up to my car to tow it away.

Obviously, I did some fast talking and prevented my car from being towed away. Then I drove Marie back to her school to pick up her car. The coffee and conversation had been great, but the parking ticket was embarrassing, especially on our first date.

It wasn't funny ten days later, when I had to appear in traffic court to pay my fine, just as anyone else would have to do. I went in my civilian clothes so as not to be recognized by any other police officers, particularly those from Central Division.

It was not until five years later that I learned that the best way to fix a ticket was to simply plead "not guilty" and go to traffic court as directed after posting the money for the bail on the citation. About 20% of the time the officer who wrote the ticket will be unable to appear in traffic court because of other court cases, vacation, late for court, or other priority activities. The traffic-court judge just simply dismisses such cases when the officer does not appear in court.

As I was naïve about the traffic-court system, I simply paid the $25 and explained to Marie that I had taken care of it.

That sounded better than "I paid the ticket" and it was certainly less embarrassing.

4

WEEKEND WARRIOR

Three months passed quickly and change-of-watch rolled around again. I was now assigned the night watch with a 3:15 p.m. roll call. Most weekdays I had to be in court by 8:30 a.m. and was usually there until noontime. Court was a drag for street cops as most cases were disposed of prior to going to trial. Cops got quite good at playing card games while their case was waiting to be called. Cards were played in the officers' waiting room, out of public view.

On the mornings I wasn't in court, I was taking flying lessons at the Compton Airport. Compton was a rough area and no one could understand why I wanted to do it there.

The reasons for using that airport were two. I had met my first flight instructor, Dick Jacobs, at an LAPD Christmas party. Dick and his wife had attended the party with his sister, who was an officer in my Police Academy class. Dick invited me to the airport for a "free introductory flight lesson." Because it was free, he knew LAPD officers could not turn him down.

The "free lesson" was the "hook" and did I get hooked. It cost me big bucks to finally get my private pilot's license, but it was worth every penny.

Because labor and land were cheap in Compton, the flight school charged six dollars an hour less than any of the nearby airports in Los Angeles County. All the planes were rented "wet," which meant the price included fuel.

The underlying reason new pilots liked to train at Compton Airport was that it was one of the few airports that did not have a control tower. New pilots thought they could fly in and out without being directed by a control tower, but they soon learned that Compton is surrounded by controlled airspace and that communicating with airport towers and the FAA's Southern California Approach was still required. Within nine months, I had my license and had logged more than 100 hours of flight time.

Before starting to fly, the day watch had spoiled me. Court seldom interfered with my social life, sleep or work. As the judge knew we were available when at work, he would just place us "on call." We could be in the courtroom within fifteen minutes if they needed us.

Night watch was supposed to have more action than any of the other watches; therefore, about half of the uniform cops in the division were assigned here. I never seemed to have any trouble finding action regardless of my watch assignment.

In addition to work, court appearances, school and flying, I found myself serving my military obligation as a "weekend warrior" with the California Army National Guard.

Many of the weekend warriors griped and grumbled during their six years of service. I made up my mind from the beginning, two years prior to joining the LAPD, that I was going to make the best of the situation. My Army basic training was at Fort Ord, California. It had been an experience I'd never forget. Four months at Fort Sill, Oklahoma's advanced individual training helped me mature on my own, away from home. I checked off each day on my calendar but I had matured much more than I thought at that time.

Almost immediately upon my return from Fort Sill, I signed up for the Army National Guard OCS program, which was later changed to the California Military Academy. This seemed like an easy way to get second lieutenant bars from the U.S. Army. However, I realized shortly thereafter that everyone had to earn those bars. My father had been a colonel during World War II and getting a commission seemed like the right thing for me to do.

One thing that really bugged me about working the night watch, going to school, and the one-weekend reserve drill a month, I seldom got Sunday off. I enjoyed having the entire weekend off just to relax and be with family and friends, and also to keep up with my flying. I found it refreshing to leave the stressful police environment on Sundays; however, I did not receive much of an uplift by attending National Guard meeting.

Our 155-artillery battery was located in East Los Angeles and our battalion headquarters was in San Pedro, some thirty-five miles away from where I lived. It was early on a Sunday morning. I crawled into the right front seat of my jeep and motioned for the first army truck, towing a howitzer, to move out. Often we would travel in a convoy to the battalion headquarters to practice field maneuvers in the large open field behind the armory and near the flood control channel.

It took forty-five minutes to drive thirty-five miles and then we were ready for combat and war games. I was still tired as I had gotten off work just six hours earlier.

After several hours of practice setting up the aiming circle and laying the howitzer everything slowed to a crawl. As I passed by the number-two howitzer I noticed that George Parker, one of the platoon sergeants, who was also an L.A. police officer, was concentrating on something as he looked through the panoramic telescope on the howitzer.

I stopped and asked, "George, what have you got?"

He backed away and chuckled, "Take a look for yourself."

I looked long and carefully and then agreed with George. He had spotted a bright yellow '57 Chrysler, parked over by the flood control basin, with two males inside who appeared to be "shooting up drugs" on government property!

George and I agreed that we couldn't pass it up. At least we had to check it out. At a minimum, it would liven up the morning. We jumped in my jeep and drove the long way around the field and stopped about fifty yards behind the suspects. To our amazement, they were so involved they didn't even see or hear us approach.

As we walked toward the car, we both felt a little unprepared. We were in U.S. Army uniforms and without weapons, handcuffs or a police radio to put out that secure "officer needs help" call, if the need arose.

We stopped at the rear of the car and eyeballed each other. The two suspects had still not spotted us. George and I shrugged our shoulders, then crept to the front doors of the car. I glanced in and saw the front seat and glove box lid covered with narcotic paraphernalia and "H," slang for heroin.

By now we were committed. I pulled out my "buzzer" and said, "Police officer. You're under arrest. Step out of the car."

Both suspects were shocked. I'm sure they had never seen a team of narcotic officers or undercover officers in Army uniforms. Our commands, badges, haircuts and attitudes were the only things that resembled the police.

The passenger suspect dropped his hype kit and exited the vehicle peacefully. The driver, who was George's suspect, opened his door, stepped out and took off running with George in hot pursuit. In that split second, as I was trying to get my strategy plotted, my suspect quickly darted to my left, then headed down and across the flood control basin with me waddling after him like a duck. Army boots were not ideal for a foot race and the suspect seemed to be faster.

My mind quickly flashed back to Mitchem and those long runs at the Academy. Maybe my endurance, not my speed, would help me to achieve victory. However, the farther I chased this guy, the farther the distance between us became. Another ten seconds and he would be long gone. My mind again flashed: Do something quickly; do something even if it's wrong; make a decision!

As a last resort, I threw out my right arm, extended it directly at the suspect, much like a turret on a Sherman tank. I carefully extended my right index finger, cocked my right thumb and yelled, "Halt or I'll shoot!"

The suspect glanced back over his left shoulder and saw I was pointing what appeared to be a gun, at him. To my amazement he stopped dead in his tracks, threw up his hands and I continued my pursuit with a flying leap onto the suspect. Five minutes later, I had this former track star back in the rear of my jeep with his hands securely fastened behind him with my army belt.

I was convincing myself that I was going to have to increase my workout program when George came back empty-handed, really puffing. He was obviously embarrassed that his guy had gotten away. I figured it was not necessary to explain to George how I bagged mine. It was just as well if George was convinced my suspect could not evade or lose me. Then I remembered the Harbor Freeway caper, Griffith Park and several other times I had been humbled by my limitations.

A few minutes later a Harbor Division police officer impounded the yellow Chrysler and booked the suspect.

Neither George nor I received any overtime on this caper. However, we did get a double hitter. Our National Guard commanding officer, Major Robert M. Snow, commended us for "service beyond the call of duty." The police reports were eventually sent to our respective police commanding officers and he wrote a favorable incident report. Both George and I concluded that these commendations were helpful to have in our personnel files when applying for a promotion.

That afternoon, as I headed back toward the East Los Angeles Armory with the trucks and howitzers following, the breeze felt good on my face. I had learned to use whatever was available to the fullest extent, even my extended finger and cocked thumb which, to this day, the suspect believed was my gun.

Several months passed and I worked my way back to a mid-p.m. watch assignment.

As Hanks would have said, "It was H and H." It really was hot and humid with temperatures above 100 degrees. My clothes were sticking to my body and dripping with perspiration. Wednesday, August 11, was indeed a day to remember. Police cars had only been equipped with automatic transmissions and heaters for a couple of years and it was unreasonable to think cops would ever get air conditioning.

I was assigned to an L unit and still liked to work alone. As the temperature was quite high, tempers flared all day. The radio clattered annoyingly with family and neighbor disputes. After what seemed to be a long day at work, I even blew my top at the cook at Tommy's Hamburgers for putting onions on my greasy chiliburger. I was scheduled to go EOW at 11:00 p.m.

Around 8:00 p.m. the communications link operator simulcast to all units, "All day and mid-watch units from 77th Street, University, Newton Street and Central Divisions, do NOT go end-of-watch. Return to your station for reassignment. We have a 'Major 415' in the Watts portion of 77th Street Division, near 116th Street and Avalon."

Prior to 1900, Watts was known as Mud Town. It was renamed for C.H. Watts, a rancher and realtor. In 1926, the city fathers annexed Watts to the city of Los Angeles. It was a small area, not much larger than one square mile. After tonight, the new city leaders might second guess their decision to annex Watts.

The Central Division units reported to the watch commander at Parker Center. He teamed the L units together to make A units, a two-officer car. In most parts of the city, only two-officer, A units were utilized. However, in Central Division and several other divisions, management used L units thereby having twice the number of black and whites available.

The police union opposed the L-unit concept, as they felt it was unsafe for an officer to operate anywhere alone in the city. High productivity had made the LAPD famous worldwide. The others wanted higher productivity and believed they received twice the coverage with L units. Sometimes I wondered if the police car did the work or the officer inside the car.

Interesting, now there was a major disturbance in the south end of the city and management was validating the police union's position by forming two-officer units to respond to the emergency. Street cops saw this was another plus for the union.

The watch commander teamed me with Richard Foster. Dick graduated one academy class behind me so I was the senior officer. I now could call the shots and give orders for the first time in my career, but was I ready for this responsibility?

By 9:00 p.m., we had our riot helmets thrown on the back seat and were southbound on the Harbor Freeway. As I was unfamiliar with 77th Street Division, I took the Manchester Boulevard exit rather than ask Foster which off-ramp to take. Of course, just as I took the off-ramp my junior partner asked me, "Why didn't you take Century Boulevard?" I hesitated, not wanting to appear inexperienced and said, "I want to get a feel of the area before I reach 116th Street." It sounded okay, but it was all "B.S."

We headed eastbound and two blocks later, at Broadway, I stopped for the signal light. Traveling southbound were twelve to fifteen black and whites, obviously moving as a unit from, I guessed, Newton Street Division. They all had their reds on and the lieutenant was in the lead car. I recognized him. It was Police Lieutenant Don Stevens, who was also a weekend warrior. Stevens held the rank of major and was the executive officer of the 186th Infantry Battalion, which was headquartered in Van Nuys. Tonight, however, Stevens was just Police Lieutenant Stevens. Newton Street was very organized and had sent their units in convoy fashion, helmets were on like tin soldiers, and the passenger officer in the front seat had his shotgun in hand and visible. I thought, that's probably military innovation by Stevens.

The non-military experienced lieutenant at Central Division had simply told us to report to Imperial Highway and Avalon. Being the senior officer and with no Central Division police lieutenant or sergeant to follow, I thought it was clever of me to follow Steven's lead by turning on my reds and joining the convoy. I suggested we put on our helmets and that Dick might want to hold and display our shotgun as Newton Street Division was doing. The practice of using a convoy was nothing new for me. Besides, I had no idea where to find Avalon and 116th Street. I certainly wasn't going to embarrass myself by asking Dick.

When we reached the command post, all the black and whites were parked as if they were in a downtown parking lot. We blocked east-west traffic on Imperial Highway. One Molotov cocktail would have wiped out twenty-five percent of the LAPD fleet. The department was as prepared for a major disturbance as the military was prepared for Pearl Harbor. Some officers wore riot helmets, some soft hats, and some no headgear at all.

A few of the sergeants from various divisions began directing their officers, but most of us just mulled around at the assembly area, which was a gas station located on the southeast corner of 116th. A 77th Street Lieutenant ordered us to stand by while the crowd threw rocks and bottles, yelled, screamed and called us "pigs." At this point no one was seriously hurt and there were only a few broken windows in the police cars.

As I waited in the command post a thought flashed through my mind. Only a few miles east and a little farther south is Compton Airport. I wondered if the disturbance would spread to that area, specifically where the Cessna 172-Skyhawk that I always rented, would be parked. I had the plane reserved for eight o'clock the next morning. It would be topped off with fuel about this time of the evening in order to ensure no condensation in the fuel tanks, which was just standard operating procedure.

Then I remembered my third solo flight when I was practicing touch-and-go landings. On my first landing, I glanced to my left and saw my instructor standing next to the flight school. He had both thumbs up, which meant he had seen the outstanding landing.

39

Feeling a little cocky and overconfident, I pushed in the carburetor heat level and jammed the throttle to the instrument panel to take off with full power and hoping to score more points with my instructor.

I kept moving down Runway 25L, which has a magnetic heading of 250 degrees and is to the left of Runway 25R. With full power the plane roared and kept moving but on the ground. It hugged the ground and I nearly panicked. Then out of the corner of my left eye I saw the flaps still fully extended. They were a full forty degrees in the "dirty" configuration. This was wrong because it meant I had too much drag and no lift. I was thankful that I had enough runway left to gradually raise the flaps in increments and gain enough lift to clear the fifty-foot obstacles at the west end of the runway. After that close call, as the P.I.C., (Pilot In Command), I stuck to the practice of always using my check list.

Tonight at 116th Street and Avalon Boulevard, there were no established check lists for the P.I.C., or incident commander. There were no instructors on the sidelines to give the thumbs-up or thumbs-down sign. We just stood around with our flaps down in the dirty configuration and could not take off. We were about to run out of runway!

We were never briefed at the scene. The rumor was that a CHP (California Highway Patrol) officer had stopped a black male who was deuced, which meant a drunk driver. Or, as we would say in court, "He violated Section 502 of the California Vehicle Code."

The arrestee had nearly made it home and members of his family and neighbors had observed the arrest. Everyone was outdoors to escape the heat and humidity inside their homes. Very few, if any, had the luxury of, or could afford fans, cooling systems, or air conditioning. They were physically and emotionally hot, and maybe, looking for some trouble or a way to vent their belief that there was social injustice. Tempers were frayed and everyone was on edge. In any case, they had refused to let the CHP officers leave the scene with their prisoner. Although this was a CHP caper, LAPD would undoubtedly take the criticism.

Communication Division called it a "Major 415." Section 404 of the penal code describes a riot as "any use of force or violence, disturbing the public peace, or any threat to us such force or violence, if accompanied by immediate power of execution, by two or more persons acting together, and without authority of law."

It was a major disturbance, an enraged group of people. Section 404 of the penal code, or whatever words you chose, this was the start of the Watts Riot. The next five days would see 34 people die, over 10,000 rioters participating, more than 600 buildings damaged by burning and looting, hundreds of people injured, millions of dollars in property damage, and more than 3,000 people arrested. The area affected by the riots covered, in the end, nearly fifty square miles or about one-tenth of the city.

As cops, we had never seen such outrage and anarchy. We couldn't believe that people would set fire to their local businesses, then loot them and overturn vehicles of innocent citizens. They were crazy!

We worked fourteen-to-sixteen hour days and seemed to lack objectives or goals. It seemed that we were only trying to survive.

On Thursday, August 12, the chief announced on TV, that the LAPD had controlled and contained the riot in a defined area. The police estimates were incorrect as Thursday wasn't over and Friday the thirteenth, hadn't yet arrived!

Just about the time the chief was finishing his TV broadcast, things started to happen at the old Watts Substation, which housed a very small police group and a fire station attached to the same building.

The rioters had a good plan, a double hitter for them. They would burn the buildings down. As the cops and firemen fled the buildings, the rioters would start shooting as there was little, or no, cover for the good guys. Two police officers were seriously injured in this incident.

On "Black Friday," we could hardly see the sky because it was filled with black smoke from the burning city. Looting was rampant. People were out of control. TV crews televised the crimes being committed. Other major cities in the U.S. had experienced such riots but the black people in those cities did not face the same problems as those in L.A. We didn't think it would happen here although there was unrest among the people.

I was scheduled for military leave from August 13 through August 27 in order to attend annual summer camp with the National Guard. I couldn't believe this. The city was burning and the governor was out of state during the entire riot. The lieutenant governor was indecisive by still not activating the National Guard to assist the LAPD and other law enforcement agencies. At noon, my phone rang. It was the watch commander wanting to know if I could report to Central Division. I explained that my military leave had started and I was to report to my military unit in two hours. He acknowledged he had forgotten about the orders already approved.

By three o'clock, I was at the East Los Angeles armory, but knew someone would not let us leave to go to summer camp with the city in trouble! At 8:00 p.m. the artillery battery commander said, "Move out." I could not believe my ears. He was as shocked as I was but the order from the battalion C.O. was, "Head for Camp Roberts," which was located in central California, some 300 miles north of L.A.

We traveled almost ten hours, in convoy, at speeds of up to forty-five miles per hour, to Camp Roberts waiting for the order to turn back to support law enforcement in L.A. However there was no "turn back" order. We were ordered to unload our equipment. We could not believe this. We were going to play war games while the city was on fire!

Finally, after everything was unloaded, tents pitched and the artillery pieces were laid, the order came. "Load up, we have been activated by the lieutenant governor and are to return to L.A. Our mission will be to support local law enforcement." By midnight we had traveled back to L.A. We unloaded and pitched our tents at battalion headquarters. This was the same training area where George Parker and I had chased the narcotic suspects several months earlier.

Saturday, August 14, was a zero for our contribution in controlling the Watts Riots due to time spent commuting back to L.A. By midday, there was almost 13,000 National Guardsmen patrolling the city. The tide was beginning to turn for the better and the police were finally getting help and relief.

On Sunday, August 15, I was sent to Division Artillery Headquarters in Northeast Los Angeles. Later, I returned to Watts, for the first time in military uniform. Things were really beginning to slow down and the governor had imposed a curfew. Maybe the rioters were just tired or there was nothing left to steal or burn? Law enforcement and the military were gaining control now.

This was a hectic day for me. My two arrests of looters were easy because the rule was that the military personnel had to immediately turn their prisoners over to active LAPD personnel. This meant they did all the paper work, not those on military status.

When cops saw another cop in a military uniform it always brought an interesting conversation. The chatter usually would start with what military organization was involved, ranks and assignments but ended up being about LAPD assignments and the latest dirt going on.

The different role never seemed to fit and yet it was ideal. Military training parallels the training police officers need and vice versa. Besides, cops receive thirty day military leave, with pay, each year. It was the ideal second job for a police officer. Military leaders liked that arrangement.

The Watts Riot officially ended on August 16. Peace was finally restored but the riots would have long-range effects on city government, law enforcement and the community at large. Burnt-out buildings, boarded-up windows and destroyed city property would remain for a long time. The scars from the riots would never completely heal.

After this, the LAPD got all the riot training its members could ever want. Every budget request was approved. Pay raises came like windfalls. Pension plan improvements were put on the ballots and the citizens always supported us. In short, we got just about anything we asked for, just like clock work.

The citizens insisted and supported increasing the department from 5,000 officers to 8,000, which meant many new promotional opportunities. L.A. cops would refer to the next fourteen years as the "Golden Years," until California's Proposition 13 was passed and ended the upward mobility of many in government service, particularly in the LAPD.

The funds for expansion in city and county government, including police departments, would quickly come to a standstill. Expansion in law enforcement meant more sergeants, more lieutenants and more captains. However, Proposition 13 would slow the growth and actually eliminate many existing promotional positions. Promotions would now be left to filling only vacancies created by retirements, if the positions were not eliminated.

5

TRAFFIC

Two years had passed since I had raised my right hand and swore to uphold the U.S. Constitution and enforce the laws of the State of California. The first and last days at the Los Angeles Police Academy were memorable occasions, but the real learning had taken place following my training at the Academy, while working a variety of jobs in Central Division.

Because of my injuries from the shooting, I remained in my first division much longer than is normally the case. This allowed me to get to know Parker Center and the people working at the LAPD headquarters.

The shooting early in my career, made me an expert in exercising officer safety, or at least I thought so. It probably made me a little paranoid, but that was good in some ways.

Officers always liked their first division of assignment because it was the first real introduction to the streets. Hanks said, "You always work harder in the first division to keep from getting your head kicked in." I was no exception to this rule and especially after the shooting.

Some of the young, more ambitious officers, had advised me to select a division where I didn't think I would like to work. It had to be a uniform job. By doing this, I would get a new job experience that looked good on my promotional application some day.

Also, there was a new department policy requiring officers to work at least three divisions prior to selecting a "home," a good place to work until retirement, if they didn't luck out and get promoted.

By selecting a division that I really didn't want to work for the rest of my career, I would be assured of getting out of there on the third transfer. This seemed like a hard way to make the system work for me but I decided to give it a try.

The mandatory transfer program was actually good for the officers and good for the department. Thinking about Higgins working in 1U2 in Central Division for twenty-three years, day-in and day-out, just didn't appeal to me. I could not see myself following in this career pattern.

After looking around I decided the least appealing uniform assignment would be working traffic. I walked across the hall to Accident Investigation Division, A.I.D., and filed a request for transfer. The next month I was a traffic accident investigator.

The traffic uniforms were more impressive with the white hats, patches on the shirts, and the useless small silver chain that hung from the right button on the shoulder and extended down to the right shirt pocket. Citizens mistakenly thought there was a whistle on the end of the chain. It was actually for looks only.

Today was May 26 but the daily activity's log showed May 27 because this was the morning watch and roll call started at 10:30 p.m. This was a bad hour to start work. I was assigned to 3T34, a two-officer investigation unit working the south end of the city. My new partner, a young officer with a five-digit serial number, was my senior by eighteen months.

Although Raul Osborne had a year and a half more experience on the job, he wasn't an old salt. It was obvious just by where he sat during roll call.

The watch commander, Lieutenant Carl Roberts, didn't have gray hairs and wrinkles. He was a young, aggressive fellow and called for an inspection that first night. I lined up near the middle of the formation in hopes of blending in, unnoticed, at least until finding out from other officers what the lieutenant looked for during inspections.

As Roberts walked in front of each officer, conducting a formal inspection, he was eyeballed. Was he going to inspect my gun? It hadn't been cleaned since qualifying two days earlier.

The lieutenant's lack of time-in-grade had also earned him his assignment to the morning watch. It couldn't have been by choice, as this watch was the most undesirable shift. It was almost impossible to live a normal life when working these hours.

He was checking weapons, at least it looked as though he would inspect about every third or fourth one. *If he doesn't inspect the guy to my right, he's bound to check mine.*

As the lieutenant reached the guy on my right, he caught a glimpse of me as he was checking his twelve rounds of spare ammunition. Darn it. There is no doubt he will step in front of me next and ask for my revolver.

Lieutenant Roberts stepped in front of me and said, "Phillips, your uniform looks great. I also want to welcome you to the morning watch as well as to Accident Investigation Division. Good to have you on our team." Roberts then stuck out his hand and shook my hand along with a flashing big smile.

After the inspection, I told Raul about my jitters over the dirty gun. I asked him if the lieutenant was always so positive in his approach with the troops. It seemed he had a very special way about himself and cared about his people. Raul described him as a good guy; however, he could get tough when necessary. Most of the officers respected him.

Two months later the nervous feeling was gone. It was late evening and we received a traffic accident call. Raul had done a good job training me in this relatively short time. For some reason Raul seemed to be up tight so I asked him what was up. He said Internal Affairs Division, I.A.D., was after him and explained that he had been ordered to go to their offices where the investigators interviewed him about the personnel complaint.

Raul, and a sergeant working Wilshire Division, had formed a business partnership to build houses. About two months earlier while working day watch, on-duty and in uniform, Raul went to the State Contractors Licensing Bureau in the state building in downtown Los Angeles. He went there to apply for their contractor's license so everything was on the "up and up."

The investigators had just sent him a copy of his statement to sign and certify as correct. That was why he was so up tight. Raul was not too bright as he listed the police department's telephone number for a contact number on the license application. He probably gave that number out of habit as police officers never give their home phone number or address; but, for an off-duty business, come on. He had five days to return the statement to the investigators.

Raul said I.A.D. would complete their investigation, submit it to his commanding officer, who would recommend a Board of Rights to the chief of police to prove he was really tough. The chief would naturally go along with the commanding officer's recommendation. The Board of Rights, consisting of three captains or above in rank, would then find him guilty of conducting a personal business on duty because of his statement. They would surely recommend the chief fire him. The chief would make an example of Raul.

The radio then sounded with, "3T34, 3T34, Ambulance T/A, Arlington and 43rd Street, Code 2."

Raul "rogered" the call and we headed south on Arlington from Washington Boulevard. Several minutes later we arrived at the address. A ten-year-old boy had been riding his bicycle without lights or reflectors and wearing dark clothing and no helmet. With no warning the boy failed to obey the posted stop sign and entered 43rd Street. East-west traffic on 43rd Street had the right of way because they did not have a stop sign.

A female teenage driver, in an old green '60 Dodge, had been clipping along, eastbound, at about thirty miles an hour and did not see the boy on the bicycle until she heard the distinct thud and then saw blood splatter on her windshield.

The bicycle was totaled and the ten-year-old boy was lying motionless on the street. A resident in the area had brought out blankets and was trying to comfort the youngster while waiting for the ambulance. Raul and I had our hands full before they arrived.

Traffic at the intersection was clogged. The congestion was not so much by the vehicle and the parties in the accident, but by curious people who were rubbernecking at the blood and guts.

We had to look at the gory injuries from the accidents as part of our job. Why would the public want to see such gruesome sights when they have an option? I'd never figure it out.

Although it was now near midnight, a crowd of spectators was forming on the sidewalk.

The driver of the car, a young black female, was standing next to her car crying profusely. "I didn't mean to, really officer, I didn't. I never saw him or the bike." She sobbed as we approached the scene after parking the police car.

Raul stopped to assist and interview her but I had hoped he would let me help her instead of the injured boy. He was now my responsibility until the ambulance arrived. *Hurry, ambulance, hurry!* This is going to be tough, no matter what.

There was a black woman, probably in her mid-forties, wearing her robe, obviously a resident of the neighborhood, leaning over the boy. "Officer, give me your belt quickly."

"What, what…?" I asked.

"Officer, I need your belt, now!" she insisted as she reached up with one blood-stained hand and held the boy's upper left leg with the other hand.

I was not going to question the woman anymore as she appeared to be much more calm and in control than I felt. She knew exactly what she was doing. I ripped off my Sam Brown belt, which held the gun, ammunition, key ring and other police equipment, then quickly pulled off my underneath belt. The lady, who obviously had extensive medical training, made a tourniquet on the boy's left leg as I fumbled trying to apply my first-aid training and assist her.

The young boy was unconscious, badly bruised and cut on his face and arms. His upper left leg was broken with extensive bleeding both internally and externally. One of the leg bones was protruding, obviously broken in several places. Although my bullet wounds were well healed, seeing the young boy's injuries brought back memories of the pain I had suffered. I now cringed inside at the sight of blood, but hid my emotions effectively.

"Are you a doctor?" I asked.

"No, I'm a registered nurse," she replied. "I work in the emergency room at Daniel Freeman Hospital."

I probably had seen her at the hospital before but I didn't recognize her in a robe with her hair up in rollers. She wouldn't win a prize in a beauty contest tonight, but her professional skills were unquestionably evident and valuable.

Now I could hear the siren of the approaching ambulance. A few minutes later, the paramedic had placed the boy on a gurney and off they sped. Code 3, to Central Receiving Hospital.

I walked Ida Mae Hooper back to her house and thanked her for her help. This caring woman had gone beyond the call of duty. She had, without a doubt, saved this boy's life.

Later, as I stood on the corner surveying the intersection, my supervisor, Sergeant Bill Hawn, parked near the south curb. He walked toward us wearing his hat as usual and appearing to be very pleased with our job. I thought, someday if I ever make sergeant, I'll have to like that hat. If I ever make chief, I'd do away with the hat altogether.

For ten minutes we discussed how the collision had occurred, how it could have been avoided and the injury that seemed so unnecessarily sustained. Near the end of the conversation we were talking about the serious injury and real possibility of death to the young victim, when Hawn said, "Phillips, you and Raul again did a good job. Keep up the good work."

"Thanks, sarge," I responded.

We spent several minutes discussing our views on life and death. Hawn stated how life is so short. It can be wiped out at any moment. He emphasized that life is precious. He concluded the conversation with another compliment for my quick efforts. He probably wanted more productivity.

After we cleared from the call, I thought about the conversation with Hawn. He was a sincere fellow. In police circles we would refer to him as a "straight shooter," meaning we could always predict his decisions. He was logical, honest and a reasonable supervisor who expected a day's work for a day's pay.

Two hours later, Raul wanted to return to Parker Center to see if he could talk the lieutenant into giving him a "special" for Monday so he could participate in an antique car show. I had initiated this by telling Raul I had lucked out the day before by scheduling a special day off on Sunday, which was really a Saturday night off.

I would take a Sunday off whenever possible but never waste a "special." I felt this was always a good investment of the hard-earned eight hours of overtime.

While Raul headed for the watch commander's office, I headed for the coffee room. Lieutenant Roberts was just leaving as I entered. He turned and said, "Phillips, how about stopping by my office before you go back to the field?"

"Sure, lieutenant," I replied.

Upon entering the office we shook hands and he extended his congratulations after reviewing the sergeant's report of the bicycle accident. We talked briefly about the incident and how it could have been prevented. He probably wanted me to write more bicycle tickets and have a detailed recap. I thanked him for his concern and taking time to talk with me.

How different the quasimilitary police department was from the Army. In the Army, a lieutenant would never be as personally open with the troops. Lieutenant Roberts had gone out of his way to show concern, yet he didn't need or want anything from me.

I changed out of my uniform and was ready to leave Parker Center after making one personal phone call to Central Receiving Hospital. I wanted to check on the boy's condition. The nurse on duty advised me that it looked as though the bicycle rider was going to pull through. I thanked the nurse and gave a sigh of relief.

At 7:00 a.m. while driving home, I thought how the job had taught me to conceal feelings, yet sincere human concern and compassion had to be part of an officer's emotions. I wondered if those feelings started when the badge was pinned on or at birth.

I pledged to myself that if Marie and I ever had children, we would never allow them out on a bicycle after dark. The bike would definitely have a headlight, reflectors and be properly equipped. I was convinced that parents who really love their children would adhere to strong discipline. My wife and I had often discussed how we would train our children in the way they should act and make decisions, so that when they grew up they would do the right thing in life.

At the academy I learned that California had about twenty-six codes that govern the people of the state. These include the penal code, vehicle code, and health and safety code, to name a few. I thought it would be so easy if parents simply followed the Ten Commandments as the way to raise and train children. Marie taught me this.

Raul said he had an easy, disciplinary system with his children. Three rules: One, do not touch my gun; two, do not go into the street; and, three, obey his other rules! The third rule was a catch-all rule to cover all of his directions. He said he dealt with his kids and though they were in "contempt of cop" if they violated his rules.

Marie felt strongly that the Ten Commandments gave rules for living, regardless of age. She said I was too dogmatic. When I told this to Raul, he said he'd think about it, but never brought the subject up again.

Three months passed on the morning watch and both Raul and I put in to change shifts to the night watch. The graveyard shift, or morning watch, was a tough watch to work. My body just could not adjust to sleeping during the day.

On the night watch, our roll call started at 3:15 p.m. and we went end of watch at midnight.

One day, shortly after 4:30 p.m., Raul and I pulled a lady over at Los Feliz Boulevard and Riverside Drive for making a left turn when the intersection was posted, "No Left Turn Between 4:00 p.m. and 6:00 p.m." Actually the location was one of my "apple orchards," a routine ticket spot, and I could write as many tickets here as I wanted. It was like picking apples in an orchard.

It was my turn to write the ticket so I walked to the driver's side and asked to see her driver's license. She was real nervous. She started giving the usual excuse that she didn't see the posted sign as most people we stopped at this location stated. As I looked at the woman, I thought I recognized her. She seemed familiar but I couldn't place her.

After a considerable delay, she finally produced her driver's license. Her name was Helen Rose Tabor and she resided in Walnut Heights. Then it hit me. This woman was my mother's best friend when they went to high school together. They had remained friends even when both had started their families. I hadn't seen her for about ten or fifteen years, but this had to be the same person. I was only a boy, about ten or twelve years old when we last spoke.

She and her family had moved to a more upscale neighborhood north of Pasadena. As I recalled, her economic status had risen by several million dollars, so she and mom had grown apart, but they still had fond memories of their friendship during their days of growing up together.

She looked at least twenty years older than I remembered her, but on the other hand, I'm sure I looked much older than the last time she had seen me. Anyway, she had not yet recognized my name tag on my uniform.

I thought maybe I'd just have a little fun with her so I said, "You know it is very dangerous to make a left turn here during these busy hours. That's why it is posted to prohibit the left turn. Also, your right rear stop light is not working. These two violations make an expensive ticket."

Naturally she said the usual, "Yes, officer. I'll never do it again."

Then I said, "I believe in mental telepathy. Do you?"

She stammered and stuttered.

As I studied her driver's license, I rubbed it between my thumb and index finger. I pretended to close my eyes and be in deep concentration.

"You attended Westboro High School in East Texas and graduated just before World War II. Then you moved to California before you were twenty years old," I said.

She replied, "Yes officer, I did!"

I continued, "You married Henry Tabor and have two children."

Helen said, "Officer, you are right!"

I couldn't resist, so I continued, "Your husband has worked many years at JPL in Pasadena. And your best friend in high school was a lady by the name of Mary Joanne Smith, who is now known as Mary Joanne Phillips."

She replied, "You are the most amazing and smartest police officer I've ever seen. How do you know all this information? It's all true."

Then I let it out, "Well, Mrs. Tabor, my name is Brad Phillips and my mother is Mary Joanne."

She couldn't believe it. With that she got out of her car and gave me a big hug and started to cry.

I walked her to the curb and she told me how happy she was to see me after so many years. Then she said that Henry had been killed six months earlier, just two days before Christmas, in a traffic accident. A drunk driver had run into him head on while he was driving home from work.

With this, I really felt terrible. I felt sick. I would never have joked with her had I known about the unexpected death of her husband.

Raul said it was probably the best thing for her, but I still felt really bad about it. I put my ticket book away and told Helen I was going to give her a "warning" this time, but next time she might not be so fortunate. It was good to see her again and she was happy to receive just the warning.

A couple of days later, it was raining "cats and dogs." Good cops always figured out how to never go hungry or get wet. In A.I.D. there were no probationary officers, so the veterans often would not show on their log that they took forty-five minutes for Code-7, free time to eat.

Don't get me wrong, the guys always took all the time they wanted, but just didn't show it on their log. Often, we could con the sergeant into letting us get off early, forty-five minutes, if we could show no Code 7 on our activity report. Just too busy to eat! If we got hungry, all we had to do was stall on clearing from a traffic accident and drive through Tommy's, McDonald's or Burger King. Or, we could do the same thing before responding to a call.

There was no reason for cops to go without eating. When it rained, cops did all interviews, if possible, in their police vehicle, in a building or engineered their "end of watch call." One thing for sure, we rarely wrote traffic tickets standing out in the rain. Keep dry and never go hungry was the goal.

Our first call out of the station was a hit-and-run misdemeanor at York Boulevard and Beach Street. When we arrived, we rolled down the window and invited the little old lady to have a seat in the rear of the police car so we could complete our traffic accident report. It was amazing how officers could write a perfect report and never get rained on. The lady thought we were nice to keep her dry.

After clearing from the accident, we were assigned a burglary silent-alarm call at the bank located on 23rd Street and San Fernando Road.

It always bugged traffic officers to get radio calls that patrol units should be assigned. Traffic units always tried to handle the traffic calls if they were assigned to patrol units. They waited until the radio operator repeated the call a second time, then I begrudgingly "rogered" the call.

When we got about two blocks away from the bank, a Hollenbeck radio car told Communications they would handle the call. I "rogered" the cancellation but we rolled on over to the bank to back up the patrol officers. The officers appreciated the backup. The patrol unit put out a Code 4, meaning no further assistance was needed. No paperwork for anyone on this call. Easy as it could be and another line for the log.

We handled five more traffic accidents, but nothing serious. When it rains, the oil comes off the asphalt and cars skid all over the place. In sunny Southern California, people don't know how to drive in the rain.

Now it was only one hour until end of watch and the communication operator chattered, "Any unit in the vicinity of 23rd Street and San Fernando Road, a burglary silent alarm at the bank. Handle the call Code 2."

Raul was driving and said, "Let's take it."

I asked Raul why in the world would we want to take the call that patrol should handle. He thought this would be a great end-of-watch call. Besides, we would get off work on time. In police work this is called *engineering the call.* Also, Raul had to finish up his review of his Internal Affairs statement. So we took the call.

In order to make the call last an hour and a half, we requested the bank manager be contacted and respond to the location. Communications made the notification to the bank manager.

We didn't even check the outside of the bank as a patrol unit had just been there seven hours earlier. Besides, 98 percent of all 459 silent alarms are false. From an officer's safety standpoint, our tactics were terrible.

Forty minutes passed and the bank manager arrived, responding in a very short time. We escorted him into the bank. He went to the vault and said it was secure. Raul asked him if we could check inside just to ensure that everything was secure. After all, two alarms in one night was excessive. Besides, we didn't want to clear from the call so quickly.

The manager opened the vault and turned on the lights. I thought I heard a noise but didn't see anyone. The suspects must have just exited the vault via a twenty-four-inch hole in the vault floor as the bank manager opened the door and entered the vault with us.

Unbelievable! These guys had tunneled one hundred eighty-seven feet from the flood control basin directly under the bank and then took a cement cutter and cut the twenty-four-inch hole in the vault floor.

There is no telling how long it took them to do such a tunnel job. It had to take weeks or months and they didn't get caught. They must have entered the vault when the first call came out, some seven hours earlier.

They probably worked seven hours using a master key or keys to open up two hundred eighty-two safe-deposit boxes. This process took them a long time and they were very systematic. The cash in the boxes totaled more than twenty-seven million dollars yet the only thing they got away with was $178,000 from the teller's drawer.

The burglars apparently had been scared off when we opened the vault door. By the time we figured out what happened they had crawled the length of the tunnel and escaped. No prints. Nothing was left but the tunnel and the twenty-four-inch hole from the vault floor.

The suspects' next step would have been to complete the opening of the last eighteen safe-deposit boxes then systematically bag the money, jewelry and other items in the boxes. If we had not been such a good traffic team, or engineered the end-of-watch call and entered the vault at the exact moment we did, the burglars would have crawled away with about $27,000,000, tax free. These guys must have really been upset at all of us for spoiling their heist.

The paperwork and time required on this burglary were mind-boggling. The Burglary-Auto Theft Division detectives took some proactive steps and located another tunnel under a different bank that had been started.

After this caper, LAPD started routine patrol of the river beds and alerted all banks and financial institutions of the suspects' M.O. As a result of this first foiled attempt and the proactive steps taken, no more tunnel jobs took place.

Immediately after discovering the burglary, the bank manager and Raul left me in the vault alone. Yes, the thought did cross my mind. No one would ever connect me with one of the teller boxes. It was just a passing thought. Honesty and integrity meant more to me than money.

The lieutenant gave us a Class A Commendation for the outstanding burglary investigation and attention to duty. He never knew Raul had figured out a great end-of-watch call that would allow us to get off work on time.

We also got five hours of overtime with all the paperwork that had to be completed. Because it earned both of us a commendation, I figured I had to help Raul now with his personnel complaint investigation.

I stayed a half hour after we finally got off. I read Raul's statement and reminded him of how often he did not log Code 7. Raul went in and checked his log for the day in question. Sure enough, he showed no Code 7 on the particular date and he had not submitted for any overtime.

I asked Raul, "Did you go to the State Licensing Board on your Code 7?"

He thought for a minute then said, "Yes! Yes! That's it. I was on my own free time."

His amendment of his statement to I.A.D. totally destroyed their case against him. At least he changed his statement from being fatal.

The end result of the personnel complaint was that Raul was suspended for seven days without pay, for failing to formally request Code 7, not logging his free time and for working an off-duty job without a work permit. Big deal!

Then the captain at Accident Investigation Division instituted a new written policy that closed the loopholes on requiring Code 7 to be formally requested and logged daily.

That's the way it works. Some cop always fouls up a good thing. Raul was the cop who messed up our good thing regarding our Code 7 past practice that had gone on for years, but luckily, he got to keep his job.

He was forever grateful for my insight. One thing was sure, he never used the police station telephone number for conducting his personal business deals. He kept his personal business private thereafter.

6

GO TO THE STATION

I was now working the late day watch at Accident Investigation Division. This was a good watch as the roll call didn't start until 10:15 a.m. I had my routine down to a science. I would put on my uniform at home, excluding the hat. Then I put my bright yellow windbreaker over the dark blue uniform shirt. This way my uniform, except the collar, didn't show and I even looked a little sporty while driving to work.

I had learned a lot from Hanks, Hardy and the other old-timers from Central, however, it had been shocking to discover that all their griping about parking had been all show for the sergeants and rookies. These shrewd guys had engineered a deal with the parking lot attendant behind Parker Center and had always been parking on city property. What a sucker I had been, but now I was one of the boys and no longer hiked from the other side of Alameda. In sixty seconds or less I could park, slip out of the windbreaker, drop ten cents in the coffee machine and hustle into the roll call room before the watch commander called my name assigning me to 11TL68. No time was wasted.

Today was an unusual day. It was Friday, December 2, and it was raining hard. As Marie prepared to go to work, she went out to get into her Ford, but discovered the right rear tire was flat. Instead, she drove "VW" and I changed the tire.

By 8:30 a.m. I was suited up and headed for work in her car and was going to get the tire repaired before reporting to work. I stopped by Lou's service station just a couple of blocks from the police station and left the car to have the tire fixed. I ran the two blocks to work so I wouldn't get soaked. Luckily there was an umbrella on the floor of the car. Traffic was bad and the streets were slick from the rain.

Again, I barely made it to roll call on time.

As usual, Sergeant Black called my name followed by 11TL68." He then paused and said, "Did your brother ever get in touch with you?"

I replied, "No."

Sergeant Black continued, "He called here twice this morning for you. You had better give him a call."

I said, "OK," and Black continued the roll.

After we were dismissed, I tried calling my brother, however, there was no answer at home. I then tried calling my folks' home and my brother answered. He had been trying to reach me since 8:30 a.m. to let me know our mother had become ill and wasn't doing well. Mother had been taken to Hoover Community Hospital and was in stable condition. The doctor felt there was no immediate need to worry.

Butterflies began stirring in my stomach as we discussed whether we should go to the hospital at that time. We decided we could not help. Mom had a bypass operation seven years earlier and we remembered she had been sick on a number of occasions, but everything always worked out all right. After all, she was only fifty-nine years old.

I showed 11TL68 clear, which meant I was available for calls. Then I headed toward Northeast Division.

As I passed a pay phone, I stopped and called Lawrence Street Elementary School. The vice principal relieved Marie long enough for her to come to the phone as I had indicated it was important. I assured her that everything would be all right and she could continue teaching the remainder of the day.

By the time I returned to the police car, my radio was chattering, "11TL68, Code 1."

I picked up the mike and responded, "11TL68, do you have a message?"

The RTO, in a disgusted tone said, "11TL68, Ambulance-TA, Avenue 60 and Monterey Road."

I "rogered" the call and headed out to the Pasadena Freeway in heavy rain. As I approached the location, I could see that the ambulance had beaten me to the call. Two passing motorists had stopped to assist getting the victim out from under the faded red VW, similar to mine. The ambulance sped away, Code 3, to White Memorial Hospital.

What a freak accident. There was only one vehicle involved. One witness said the young woman had just weaved to the right and run off the roadway, then her car turned over, landing on top of her. She had seat belts in her car but as was so common, she was not using them.

In twenty minutes I finished at the scene and was driving to White Memorial Hospital. Upon arrival, a young nurse informed me that the twenty-three-year-old woman was nine months' pregnant and was in critical condition. The doctors were going to take the baby from the mother but first needed to reach the husband. I informed her that the husband had been notified at his office and was on his way.

The husband arrived shortly. The doctor talked with him and I stayed in the background as long as I could.

One thing that really stuck with me was that the husband repeated twice how he wished Sherry had not driven during her last month of pregnancy. She apparently passed out while driving, probably due to labor pains and ran off the roadway. Then the car overturned and because she was not wearing her seat belt, she was thrown out her door when she started rolling over and was severely crushed by the roof of the car. What a senseless accident. Why didn't she use her seat belt?

Later, as I stood in the nurse's office, I looked through the large glass window and down the corridor a short distance. I could see into the small hospital chapel and observed the husband kneeling at the altar.

As I prepared to leave, Doctor Sanders gave it to me straight. If Sherry lived, she would be a "vegetable." She would never regain consciousness as there was severe brain damage.

Walking to the car, I concluded that there were situations worse than death. I sat in the car and leaned my head back on the headrest as I thought about Sherry, her husband and their new baby.

I thought how fortunate I was to have had my mother for twenty-five years. Sherry's baby would never know its mother.

Because it was still raining, I knew as soon as I cleared I would be assigned another traffic call, so I just sat there and looked at the rain hitting my windshield. I thought about my mother and how hard she had worked for her husband and her children.

Perhaps two minutes of daydreaming and reminiscing had passed when Karen, the young nurse, tapped on the passenger's window of my police car. She got drenched while I unlocked the door. She jumped in and slammed the door shut. I then realized that not all the water drops on her face were from the rain. In a slow, carefully worded statement, she informed me that Sherry had passed away but the new baby boy was all right.

"Passed away," sounded so much softer than "dead," but either way, the baby was without a mother.

Trying to console myself, as well as Karen, I thought, we never know. It is out of our control. Both of us played our roles pretty well. That is, we concealed our true emotions.

The information that Karen gave me could be condensed into one line on the bottom of the traffic report with two additional check marks and, of course, the simple one-page death report that meant "the end" for Sherry.

I showed the 11TL68 clear and, to my amazement, didn't get another traffic accident call. Instead, the RTO said, "11TL68, go to the station."

My mind raced with a number of thoughts.

"Go to the station," was an unusual call for a traffic unit on a rainy day. There had to be accidents all over the city and patrol units went crazy if they had to handle a simple traffic accident call. Sometimes, patrol units would be assigned a traffic call and the traffic officers would wait a short time before advising Communications they would handle the call. It was like playing a game. The patrol officers were relieved and happy and the traffic officers felt like heroes. I continued on to the station but wondered, why?

Only three blocks from Parker Center I spotted a traffic accident in the intersection. I debated whether or not to whip a U-turn or just turn my head. Finally I did what I knew was the right thing. I stopped and went out for investigation by notifying Communications Division, "11TL68, Code 6 at Los Angeles Street and Aliso, on a traffic accident."

A little old lady, who should have stopped driving a couple of years earlier, was westbound on Aliso Street making a left turn to southbound Los Angeles Street. She used poor judgment in making her turn and connected with an eastbound sporty red Mustang.

The young man driving the Mustang didn't have a clue about what heavy rain did to stopping distance. The street was like a skid pan, but he thought it was a race track as he clipped along with his Elvis tape blaring and keeping time to the music. Doing about forty-five

MPH in a twenty-five MPH zone in this rain was dangerous, even without his music. Two good witnesses attested to the facts of the accident.

Both drivers were fortunate as neither were injured, however, the lady was traumatized. A thousand dollars of body and fender work would make each car look like new again.

Both drivers would, I hoped, exercise safer driving habits for at least a month, then probably return to the old ones again. A traffic ticket or traffic accident always seemed to get their attention for at least a short time.

Police officers working traffic always wonder why drivers didn't slow down when driving in the rain. *Why don't people think?*

Twenty-five minutes passed. This accident was investigated and I was walking into the watch commander's office at Accident Investigation Division.

I caught the graying lieutenant off guard as he looked up from his desk and stuttered, "Phillips, uh, Brad," and pushed his glasses back on his nose.

The room became silent, uncomfortably silent. I could have heard a pin drop. Sergeant Black and the lieutenant stared at one another for a second, which seemed like five minutes to me. My mouth was dry again and I knew something was wrong.

I blurted out, "Did my brother call again?"

"Uh, Uh," the lieutenant stuttered again.

With anxiety obviously haunting me, I looked the lieutenant directly in the eye and asked, "Is my mother all right?"

With that, there was no more room for stuttering or evading the question. The lieutenant replied, "I'm sorry. She just expired."

I bit my lip and fought back tears as the two supervisors stood up and approached me.

"I'm okay. I'm okay. I'll call my brother," I stammered as I turned to go out of the office.

Both supervisors wanted to help, but there was nothing they could do. I repeated, "I'm okay. I'm going to call my brother."

All I really wanted to do was get away by myself so I could just cry my heart out.

"Why, oh why, didn't I go to the hospital to be with mom two hours sooner. Why?" I asked myself.

Passed away, expired, died, they all meant "dead."

In the most obscure restroom in the basement of Parker Center, I washed my face over and over again. I tried to get the crying out of my system. I was really hurting.

An officer walked in and said, "Boy, is it wet outside!"

I muttered, "Yeah. It is," as I wiped the water from my face with a paper towel making sure I concealed my tears.

I called my brother again, but everything had already been said. I left my hat in my locker, checked in my police vehicle and equipment, slipped into my yellow windbreaker, and headed for Lawrence Street Elementary School. Things were beginning to fall into true perspective. Real priorities seemed to surface. The thoughts I had when I got the call to go to the station seemed unimportant now.

The rain had subsided by now. While driving to Marie's school, I thought about all the deaths of the police officers that had occurred since I had been on the LAPD. One haunted me. This was the untimely death of my classmate who had shared a locker with me at the academy.

He was a happy man when he got assigned to motors. Riding the two-wheel police motorcycle was great for Ron, but six months after being assigned to the bike, he was wiped out by a deuce on Forest Hill Drive while writing a traffic ticket to a teenage boy for doing seventy-two miles-per-hour in a forty-five miles-per-hour zone. Ron's death earned him a formal military-type police funeral. Also, his name would be engraved on the marble L.A. Police Memorial Foundation Monument in front of Parker Center.

Then I thought how close I had come to death in my shooting incident. I had pain, but now I was alive and my mother was dead.

As I slowly walked to the top of the steps at the school, Marie spotted me through her open classroom door. She apparently read grief all over my face as she quickly gave the students an assignment and stepped outside, closing the door. She embraced me as she saw tears that I could no longer control, no matter how hard I tried.

I didn't have to explain my feelings as she had lost her father the year before. She said she would make arrangements with her principal to leave for the remainder of the day and then meet me at my parents' home.

Returning to Parker Center, I slowly completed the reports on the three traffic accidents that I had investigated earlier. The watch commander insisted they could wait but I felt I had to personally finish the reports. I needed time to unwind before joining my family for this sad occasion.

My family would need strength and support from my mother's oldest child. They viewed the cop in the family as strong with extra strength to share. That was the outward image, but inside I was hurting. I needed an hour or so to compose myself and gain some strength of my own.

My mother's death was a very difficult time for me. This afternoon I would have to make her funeral arrangements and make the other unpleasant decisions in connection with her death. I needed a little time to get control of myself and to get a clear mind.

Three days later our family was sitting in the Chapel of the Heavens at the Forest Hills Cemetery. Then I wondered why it took a death to bring our entire family together and of one mind.

Everyone always seemed to be doing their own thing and didn't have time for one another. We all had other, higher priorities.

There were a lot of our friends in attendance to give us their support. I concluded it was times such as this that one could determine who were friends and who were acquaintances. During the hour-long funeral service I did a lot of thinking about life and setting some new priorities.

7

STREET COPS

In 1984 the Summer Olympic Games were held in Los Angeles. The LAPD performed as a world-class department. The chief awarded each officer on the payroll a ribbon to wear above the right pocket on the uniform shirt. The ribbon could be worn with military ribbons earned. Street cops liked the recognition.

However, more important, twenty-one officers had died in the line of duty since Brad Phillips had entered the L.A. Police Academy. Statistically, that was more than two each year, about one every six months. It was a dangerous career.

Henry Ray, the twenty-first officer to die in the line of duty was an outstanding officer. Some big dope deal went sour and Henry took a fatal bullet in the torso. Since he was working plain-clothes narcotics, he did not have the benefit of wearing a bulletproof vest.

Henry was bright, energetic and loved his family and police work. His peers loved him. He was a devoted family man with two small children. The newspapers referred to Henry as an African-American or black. His brother officers referred to him as blue, not black. LAPD blue.

The first night we worked together was at Central Division. He had about nine months less time on the job, but as rookies, nine months is a lot of seniority. However, it didn't make any difference to Henry or me. We both liked police work and were young and energetic.

I said, "Henry, do you want to drive or keep books?"

Henry knew I was being nice and replied, "No, you drive."

Remember, street cops really do not like to do paper work. Experience taught us that driving took less effort and we commanded the police unit from the driver's seat.

Before we could get to the gas pumps, we received a Code 3 call, just a few blocks away at 7th and Main Street. It ended up being a false alarm, but that got us off to a good start.

Over the next deployment period, Henry and I worked together most of the time. He really encouraged me to study hard for promotional exams. I remember he said, "Don't be satisfied just being a street cop even though many officers are and do quite well."

Four years after we worked Central Division together, I ran into Henry at the academy while qualifying at the range. He was happy that he had just been selected to work with the Narcotic Division.

Most Los Angeles cops live out of the city, but not Henry. He lived in the Cedar Ridge area of the city. Working narcotics was an exceptionally dangerous assignment. Henry thought he could get dope off the streets and it would build a better community for his children to grow up in. He was a dedicated cop.

Who would ever figure nine years after that first false alarm call at 7th and Main Street, I would be attending Henry's funeral. At the funeral, I felt so much sympathy for his wife and two small children. I thought back to how I felt when I lost my mother.

The Los Angeles Police Memorial Foundation would help the family. They would provide assistance with the funeral, help with the children's education and other financial matters, but they could never replace Henry.

When I returned to work the lieutenant had done some research into Los Angeles police shootings. He told us during roll call that during the past twelve months, there were 152 shooting incidents with 460 shots fired by LAPD officers. Unfortunately, we only hit our target with 85 of our shots. Also, he told us that of the 256 suspects involved, 205 were captured, 51 escaped, 40 were wounded and 12 were killed. On the other hand, 64 shots had been fired at LAPD officers with only three hits. Unfortunately, one of the hits was Henry.

We discussed these findings during roll call in hopes of preventing any of us from being killed. The officers understood the subject matter very well. It was a serious subject and there were no smart remarks during roll call discussion, not even from the old salts in the rear of the room. Police officers make light of some things, but they know when seriousness is demanded, especially from their peers.

Physical harm is a reality that everyone accepts, but most people do not recognize the emotional harm an officer often suffers. Cops often see things which are enough to traumatize a normal person. Cops may laugh about some things that are gruesome. The public sees such laughter or conduct and interprets it as insensitivity to a situation. Yet this is the way officers control their emotions.

There was a horrible fire involving four young men in a drug deal. One of the first officers to arrive at the location kept referring to the horrendous scene and haunting memory of the burnt bodies as "crispy critters." At first I thought the officer was being insensitive to the situation but two days later he committed suicide. His wife said the pressure and mental anguish over what he had seen was more than he could deal with. I thought I knew the man well, but he concealed his feelings to his breaking point.

The suicide did not qualify for the classification of "killed in the line of duty." His name would not be engraved on the L.A. Police Memorial. He would soon be forgotten. Regardless, as far as I was concerned, his mental breakdown was due to his work in the line of duty.

Despite the high level of stress for all of us, real job satisfaction came when I worked as a street cop. One night I was working with Hicks, an "old timer." We were traveling southbound on Main Street at about 4:00 a.m. Hicks, as usual, was driving and I was keeping the books.

In Los Angeles, that time of the morning is really chilly. Actually, it gets cold and fog hangs near the street level. As we passed 16th Street, I glanced to my left and saw a car parked at the north curb heading westbound. I saw another vehicle traveling westbound. It was several car lengths behind the parked car.

In a flash something struck me as odd. In court, police officers are required to describe the unusual observations to justify probable cause to investigate. In this case, my momentary observations included smoke rising up from the exhaust near the rear of the vehicle. This was visible for just a split second as the moving westbound car's headlights reflected on the parked car. I saw what I believed was a silhouette of a person quickly lean from the front passenger seat to the bottom of the driver's seat. All of this probable cause to investigate in itself did not constitute a crime, only a reason to check further. All of the observations took place in about three seconds. I told Hicks, "Go back!"

Hicks made a traditional police U-turn as though we owned the street. Then we went eastbound on 16th Street, passed the parked car and whipped another U-turn, finally coming to a stop behind the parked car. The car was running as the exhaust smoke was obvious. We went Code 6 with the communication operator, which meant we were out for investigation.

As we approached the parked car, a black man raised himself up in the driver's seat. He was now sitting behind the steering wheel. We checked him and the car out but came up with nothing. I still wasn't satisfied and told Hicks it didn't make sense. I was sure that during my split-second observation, the man in the car moved from the passenger seat downward toward the driver's seat, as if he may have been hiding from us when we passed. Why did he move over to the driver's seat?

I suggested to Hicks that maybe there was another suspect who was driving the car and that he got out and was burglarizing a business in the area. With that Hicks handcuffed both hands of the suspect to his car door post. I began to check out the businesses in that area.

With little effort I located a bar across the street with the front door ajar. State law required all bars to close at 2:00 a.m.

I motioned to Hicks, who immediately called for backup. Apparently the head police photographer who worked for the *Los Angeles Examiner* newspaper heard the call for backup. He arrived first as he was just around the corner. His police radio monitor was so loud, he blew any surprise element we might have had.

Because the first suspect was securely handcuffed to his car and could not go anywhere, Hicks and I entered the bar. We should have waited for our backup, but decided to go on in.

After we searched the bar, I spotted a ceiling tile that was slightly ajar. We ordered the suspect to come down from the attic but there was no response. I stepped up on a chair, then onto a table and stuck my head into the attic area with my flashlight and gun in my hand. Almost immediately, I spotted a large man crouched down in the attic about two feet from my head. He startled me as I came face to face with him. I wasn't really expecting to find anyone. I knew then I would have to change my underwear after this caper. This was worse than an Alfred Hitchcock movie. It was scary!

I yelled for the suspect to freeze and put his hands up or I would blow his head off. This really was unnecessary as the crawl space was so small, but he couldn't move. I dropped my flashlight and grabbed the suspect by the shirt in his chest area and pulled him to the floor as we both fell.

Hicks just stood there and laughed as we lay on the floor. Of course he had the suspect covered with the department shotgun. The suspect was not hurt, but was frozen with the barrel of the shotgun in his face.

We booked both suspects for burglary and grand theft auto as the car ended up being stolen from the state of Florida. However, the stolen car had not been entered into the NCIC, National Crime Information Center, properly. We were fortunate to have not been put in harm's way with such a clerical mixup.

To our surprise, the suspect we found in the parked car admitted to both the burglary and the grand theft auto. The other suspect continued to lie and deny anything to stall or delay, but that's their way: anything to avoid justice.

Everything was unusually quiet in the neighborhood where I lived. We had good neighbors and we tried to be good neighbors. Roy and Robin Carter lived on the south side of us. I remember the hot day we moved into the neighborhood. Robin brought a tray with milk, cookies and a beautiful bouquet of flowers, just to welcome us. She was a little shy, but she was as nice and sincere as she could be.

Roy and Robin had seven children that were older than our boys. The family placed a great deal of emphasis on family values, long before Dan Quayle thought up the concept. They were devoted Mormons and went to church at least once a week. I never could understand how a man could afford to have seven children, but they handled it well. I was amazed. Roy was a great neighbor and a real friend.

Roy and his brother owned a large air-conditioning business and did installations and repairs all over Southern California. He did quite well. I admired his business knowledge and he knew how to stretch the tax dollars. He knew how to get great fringe benefits from his business and referred to them as 100% money. Later I learned that legitimate business expenses saved you about 50% in taxes.

Our house backed up to the Rio Mesa River, which was really a flood control channel in Whittier. My driveway and garage were next to the Carters' driveway and garage. Only a strip of grass and flowers separated them. This meant we had to have more contact with the Carters' than the family on the other side of our home.

Although Roy always drove a new company car, Robin could care less about new cars. She had a six-year-old, yellow Ford Bronco with 90,000 miles. The car did not have push-button windows, electric door locks or an automatic transmission, but her seven children loved the old car.

Maybe the reason she could care less about a car was because her wealthy parents always drove a brand-new Rolls Royce every year of her childhood. Of course she never considered the fact that her dad owned the dealership! The mother and father were never around as Robin and her younger sister were growing up.

Robin told Marie her parents always fought and she wanted a good relationship with her children. To Robin, this was more important than money. She was an ideal mother who loved her children greatly. Roy was a caring father. They spent a lot of time with their kids.

Roy kept his house immaculate. Everything was in its place, but one night he got in over his head and everything broke loose.

It was around 8:00 p.m. and I was stretched out on the couch watching television. The police report would read 2005 hours. Marie came running into the family room after going out front to pull the car into the garage. She yelled at me, "Brad, something is happening in front of Robin's house. Come quickly!"

I jumped off the couch and ordered her to "Get my gun!" I ran to the front door without my shoes on. As I stepped onto our dark, unlit front porch, Marie blew my cover and concealment by flipping on the porch lights. Now the world could see help on the way: not a good tactic if one plans to catch a carjacker, especially if one's unarmed.

Just as Marie turned the porch light on, I looked in the direction of the disturbance. I could see Roy in his driveway, on the driver's side of Robin's Bronco, trying to pull a large black man out of the driver's seat. Roy was yelling at the top of his voice, "Were you trying to kill her?"

As I darted across our lawn, barefooted, toward the passenger's door of the car, I saw Robin lying on the grass in front of their house. She was probably thrown to the ground from the driver's seat by the suspect. She was crying and screaming, "Just take my car and money, but don't hurt us!"

I guess Roy figured he had worked too hard to let the old car and Robin's purse go without a fight. A thought quickly went through my mind, Roy, why not just let your insurance company buy Robin a new car? Maybe a Chevy Suburban or Blazer, but instinctively, I ran to the rescue.

As I reached the passenger door of the Bronco, I yanked the door open and jumped in. I suddenly realized Marie had not brought me my gun as I had clearly requested. Then I wondered if anyone had called 9-1-1 without my telling them.

Roy was now trying to pull the man out of the driver's side while Robin was trying to pull Roy away. Maybe by now the insurance deal sounded good to Robin.

The Bronco was running and the suspect was struggling to get the stick into reverse gear. The suspect must not have been very selective of the cars he was hijacking. He sure didn't know this one had a stick shift because he wasn't proficient at shifting it. He "ground a pound" while putting it into reverse but finally succeeded.

As he jerked the clutch and moved backward, he pushed Roy back to the grass with his left hand while swinging at me with his right fist.

I told the suspect he was under arrest. He told me to get lost and was not impressed that I was an off-duty police officer. During this ordeal I was swinging fiercely at the suspect but he was so big and tough, my fist just bounced off his face. This guy was ready to eat me alive. He had to be high on coke or some other type of dope as his strength was astounding.

By now, I was left alone as Robin and Roy had retreated into the garage. They might as well have been waving goodbye to the Bronco, Robin's money, purse and me as the suspect drove away at a high rate of speed. I was punching away in the front seat as the suspect drove westbound. I hoped Marie, or at least Roy and Robin, would call 9-1-1.

After we were about half a block away and turning about 8,000 RPMs in first gear, the suspect had to shift into second gear. I thought, if I catch this guy, it will be because he cannot drive a stick-shift vehicle, not because I was such a good fighter or so tough.

If Marie had delivered my gun as requested, I could have controlled this incident, but too late now. Then all of a sudden he failed to negotiate the right turn and slammed head into a telephone pole. The suspect fell forward and hit his head on the windshield. His head was bleeding above his nose and eyes. I hit my right rib cage on the steering wheel. My ribs hurt terribly and my old bullet wound once again caused me some pain.

Luckily for me someone had called 9-1-1. A police patrol unit pulled up with red light and siren blaring. They arrived just after we crashed and took the suspect into custody.

The suspect was an ex-con on parole. Tonight he was a carjacker, high on dope, with a lacerated face. The one good ending to this incident was no one was seriously injured and all the Carter's possessions were returned.

A short bit of investigation put the story together. When Robin returned to her Bronco at the supermarket, two men in a dark blue, four-door Mercury followed her home. When she pulled into her driveway, one of the men ran up to her unlocked passenger's door. The other suspect that had been watching the fast-moving incident simply drove off after the crash.

As I approached the house, Marie was standing with a worried look on her face. I yelled at her, "Honey, why didn't you get me my gun?"

Her response was, "Brad, you know your gun is locked up in your gun locker in the closet. You have the only key in your pocket." With that, I let the matter drop.

Later, I advised Roy to buy Robin's next car with power door locks and equip it with a cell phone. I suggested Robin keep the doors locked at all times and blare the horn if something like this ever happened again. Also, I admonished her never to open the locked door under these circumstances.

A month later Robin got a new Blazer.

While working the morning watch at Newton Division, we had a horrendous take over robbery. This caper justified the division's nickname of "Shootin' Newton."

71

At 4:00 a.m. every day the manager and six stock clerks arrived at the Big Eagle Home Supply Store at Alameda and Maple Street.

Every morning the manager opened up the large safe and counted $300, in various denominations and coins for each of the twenty-two cash drawers. When the cashiers arrived for work, all they had to do was verify the cash-drawer count and carry the drawer to their assigned check-out stand. The Big Eagle was ready for business. The six stock clerks worked diligently to ensure all shelves were fully stocked before the store opened.

After setting up the cash drawers, the manager verified all receipts from the previous day and prepared all the necessary paperwork for the 8:00 a.m. armored truck pickup. The pickup took place every morning, except on Sunday when the armored truck company was closed. Monday morning was always the heaviest money day for Big Eagle as they had all the receipts for both Saturday and Sunday sales.

The armored truck pickup was like clock work. We could always predict their action as the three guards had covered almost all their security bases. One of the guards was equipped with an Ithaca shotgun and carried double-ought buck rounds, just as we had. I think robbers feared the Ithaca shotgun with the double-ought buck more than the LAPD.

Anyone watching the store for two weeks could calculate their arrival, procedure and departure. They would also conclude the best time to rob Big Eagle was before the armored truck arrived on a Monday morning, sometime between 4:00 a.m. and 7:00 a.m. The earlier the better. It would take a street-wise, sixteen-year-old kid at Juvenile Hall about five minutes to draw the same conclusion.

On Monday, June 16, the manager and crew were shocked and startled to be confronted by two hard-core, male, gun-wielding robbers, waiting inside the store.

Unbeknown to the employees, the two suspects had gone to the rear of the store at about 3:00 a.m. They climbed the chain link fence on the south side of the building and then scurried up the roof drain pipe. They hauled their automatic weapons and a sharp ax up to the roof by using a rope.

After arriving on the roof, they went to an exact location on the roof, directly above a high fertilizer storage rack and marked it with a three-foot-by-three-foot square to chop a neat hole.

They took the sharp ax and cut the hole in the roof. Afterward, they stepped down through the hole onto the top of the fertilizer rack. Their interest was not in the fertilizer to grow vegetables in their garden, but rather to increase their monetary wealth by more than a million dollars.

After entry, they worked their way down the rack to the floor, walked seventeen steps due west, then thirty-two steps north, grabbing a bag of chocolate chip cookies from aisle number twenty-six and waited for the employees' 4:00 a.m. arrival. The route they took was perfect, well-planned. The roof entry avoided the hard-wire alarm and the forty-nine steps eluded the two motion detectors in the store. They had plotted and planned their crime very well. It was obvious they had studied the interior of the store extensively and over a period of time.

The two suspects devoured the bag of cookies while waiting. At this point, the two had only committed an armed burglary. However, soon the crime would escalate.

One suspect immediately slammed the butt of his AR-15 weapon in the face of one of the young male employees. They yelled at all seven employees to lie down on the floor. Blood was all over the place due to the injury to the young fellow they had smashed in the face. They also chipped off two of his front teeth.

Later we established the approximate time of entry based on observation of the local newspaper deliveryman. He has seen a suspicious-looking van enter the lot at approximately 3:00 a.m., but thought nothing of it until the incident.

The burglary's crime now became robbery and assault with a deadly weapon. It was now a serious felony. The robbers were dressed in military-type shirt and pants, army boots, gloves, and wore ski masks, and both carried an automatic weapon and a pistol. Each suspect also had a walkie-talkie-type radio.

One suspect grabbed the manager and a female employee. He took them at gun-point into the manager's office about thirty-five feet from the front door. The large safe was in his office. Here, the manager was threatened. The suspect said the female employee would be shot in her left knee, then the right knee, then the suspect would shoot her in the head and kill her. The suspect threatened he was going to go one by one to all of the employees in the same manner. Finally, if he didn't open the safe, they were going to kill the manager and forget about the money.

With that admonition, the manager quickly opened the safe and told the robber, "Take it all!"

Naturally the suspect agreed, however, they made one costly mistake at Big Eagle.

The suspect guarding the five employees on the floor ordered the young kid, the one he had butted with his AR-15, to go to the first checkout counter and get five large heavy-duty black plastic checkout bags. That simple task would prove to be the tragic mistake.

The store clerk staggered to the checkout counter and grabbed four of the large bags, then reached down for the fifth bag. In a split second, he did it. He pushed the little black button hidden under the counter near the edge of the bag shelf.

There was probably not one of the other employees who had the intestinal fortitude to push the button if given the opportunity. They were scared to death. The suspect simply picked the wrong employee to get the bags.

The suspect thought he had picked the weakest employee. He picked an aggressive teenager, only five-feet-seven-inches tall, who had the guts of a tough Marine. This kid was upset and he knew his girlfriend was not going to appreciate the damage the suspect had done to his two teeth. So, he just pushed the button, which was not noticeable in the store.

Pushing the button sent the silent robbery-in-progress alarm to the alarm company who, in turn, relayed it to the LAPD communications center on a priority line. This took about twenty seconds.

The quiet police radio at that time of the morning sounded with a high tone *beep-beep,* followed by "All units in the vicinity of Big Eagle Home Supply Store at Alameda and Maple Street, 211 silent, 13A61 handle your call Code 2."

When the call came out, 13A61 with Paul Sanchez and Phil Osaka, and my partner Ted Ratcliff and I, were sitting in our cars next to one another at the donut shop at Alameda and Wall Street. This was only three blocks from Big Eagle. We were assigned to 13A93 and we were just finishing a cup of coffee.

Ted, who was keeping our books, told Paul and Phil we'd back them up, which meant 13A61 would have to do the paperwork. They gave the macho LAPD nod by raising their head back, which meant okay.

Normally, an LAPD unit would not be at the scene for this type of call for at least five minutes, but timing and location are everything and we just happened to be around the corner. Within thirty seconds, 13A61 was sitting in the Union 76 gas station across the street from Big Eagle, with their lights off and the radio's volume turned down low so they could scout the location.

We notified Communication to show us Code 6 at the location with 13A61. This let them know we were already there and out for investigation. We switched our radio to Tactical Frequency 2 so we could chatter with any other unit responding to the location.

Phil reported that he spotted a dark brown GMC van sitting to the extreme right of the store with its lights off. They also noted that the vehicle was running as there was visible exhaust emitting from the rear of the van. They observed what appeared to be a driver sitting behind the driver's seat. The parking lot was dimly lit, but the reflection of the poor lighting was enough to see the exhaust fumes and a person in the driver's seat.

Our plan was for 13A61 to take the north side of the parking lot and building, and we would take the south side of the parking lot and building. Paul and Phil wanted to move in quickly, but because of my memorable experience in Griffith Park, I insisted that we request for and wait for 13A43 to arrive as another backup. My decision now always went in favor of overstaffing a tactical situation and going slowly instead of rushing into this perilous type of call.

The reason cops get lax on such calls is because about 98% of them are false. We grow complacent, unless we have taken a bullet or two. Ted thought I was a little paranoid until he saw the van creeping slowly toward the front door with its lights off. From our position, it looked as though the driver of the van was talking on a hand-held radio. We learned later that he was. The two suspects inside had been tipped off that two LAPD units were now at the two corners of the parking lot awaiting their move.

The seven employees inside the store heard the chatter from the suspect's radio and knew LAPD was outside, but six of the employees didn't know how we had been notified of the robbery in progress.

75

By now we had moved closer and couldn't wait for 13A43's arrival. It was going down now and we could not wait any longer. We positioned ourselves about sixty feet from the front door of the store near the corner of the building, so we could see anyone exit the store and enter the van.

Suddenly, the front door flew open and the two suspects from inside came running out with the big black money bags in their hands. They jumped in the open sliding door on the right side of the van.

The van's driver accelerated toward us and just as they passed our position the two suspects that had entered the van, opened fire from the open sliding door with their AR-15, as they passed us. The military-type weapons they used fired several bullets that went clear through our police vehicle in several parts, but not through the engine. We were lucky to be on the driver's side of our police car, stooped down near the front tire where the motor afforded us the cover we desperately needed.

We carefully returned fire and immediately broadcasted, "Shots fired and officer needs help at the Big Eagle!"

As they got about fifty feet farther south of our position, 13A43 came driving in and blocked their exit. The van swerved to the right to avoid colliding with the police vehicle, but hit the light pole in the parking lot, which caused them to stall out. All three of the suspects jumped out of the van via the opened sliding door on the right side of the van. The suspects had evaded 13A42, but now they were on foot running toward us as they spread out.

Four other officers and I fired sixty-three shots at the suspects with our handguns and missed. The three suspects fired ninety-two shots with their automatic weapons and pistols. It sounded like the fireworks on the Fourth of July. Not one of these shots hit anyone, but they did a lot of damage. The coroner later told us that only three shots fired by my partner Ted, from the Ithaca shotgun, hit the suspects. The double-ought buck did the job.

The score was three to zero with "Shootin' Newton" victorious. Big Eagle Supply Store got their five black bags along with the 1.6 million dollars inside.

As a result of our good work, Big Eagle made a large contribution to the L.A. Police Memorial Foundation. They also gave a lot of free press for the Memorial Foundation in their weekly advertiser.

From then on, the Big Eagle always supported the Newton Division Annual Golf Tournament. They routinely filled two or three of the foursomes, sponsored a couple of the tees and gave door prizes. They were really supportive.

All the guys at Newton chipped in and we paid for the young fellow who pushed the little black alarm button, to get his two front teeth capped. He was a good kid and three years later he became a LAPD cop.

There was no cost to the taxpayers in trying or incarcerating these three robbers. All three were dead. All had been in and out of prison for the past fifteen years, but they had never learned that the "law always catches up with you."

8

WALKING THE BEAT

In the early 1800s, Sir Robert Peel, the founder of what we know today as the modern police, developed a system to divide up a given geographic police district into areas and assign officers the responsibility for that geographical area. The smallest zone, or area of responsibility, was identified as a "beat." As the officer was on foot, it was called a "foot beat."

The officer walked the area and knew the people who lived and worked on his beat. He knew the good citizens, the problem kids and the criminals. It was the most effective type of police work ever devised, however, it was the most expensive.

Police administrators who followed the methods of Sir Robert Peel learned that police productivity could be increased by making the officer more mobile. Horses, bikes, cars, motorcycles and helicopters allowed the officer greater mobility. The police radio provided communication and quicker response.

The increased mobility and freedom of the officer took away the basic strength of the foot beat, the people factor. He would no longer possess the inside knowledge about the citizens in his area. He no longer knew who was good, bad and indifferent.

In all fairness to the issue, New York City grew vertically due to lack of land, whereas the city of Los Angeles seemed to grow horizontally. We had plenty of underdeveloped land and room to expand. At the time, it was more economical to go outward instead of building large skyscrapers.

Suddenly, during the 1980s as L.A. began to grow upward and started to get its first really tall buildings, some police administrator had a great idea. Let's have officers walk a foot beat in downtown Los Angeles. They would get to know the people on the beat and help drive down the crime rate in this most influential business and commercial area.

Foot beats were set up all over downtown Los Angeles, but more importantly, the wealthy business owners were then off the chief's back. They got what they wanted.

I thought to be a foot beat officer would be an interesting assignment and a change of pace from the black and white radio car. With my seniority, the assignment would be mostly day watch with most weekends off. This meant more time with my family and more time to fly.

By now, I had met Keith Willard at the Compton Airport. Keith owned 20,000 acres of fertile land in Ventura County, where he was an absentee avocado rancher. Actually, about all he did was count money and fly. He had a home that would be considered by most cops to be a mansion. His "in-town condo" was in Torrance, but he hangared his new Cessna-182 at Compton. Keith claimed he parked his plane at Compton because it was an uncontrolled airport and that it was cheaper. He liked to say, "I don't hate my money!"

The reality was he didn't like the airport manager at Torrance because he had talked down to him on a couple of occasions.

I considered Keith as my adopted uncle. He treated me like family and let me fly his airplane all the time. He insisted that I was his director of security for his airplane and ranch and that my use of his plane was to repay me for my security services. In reality, he was very generous to me and a good friend.

Keith and I flew over three hundred hours together in his plane during the first two years of our friendship. We always split the time as pilot-in-command. The Cessna-182 had a variable pitch prop and was classified as a high-performance aircraft as it had over 200 horsepower.

This foot beat assignment was really interesting and different. I thought it would give me a new perspective on police work. My partner, Randy O'Rilley, became my best friend. He had seven years' seniority on me and we got along well. He was a big Irishman, six-foot-three-inches tall and weighed about 240 pounds. He had huge hands and a soft heart like that of a Teddy Bear.

Our sergeant gave us direct, simple orders. Keep the business owners happy and don't get hurt. We understood him well.

Both Randy and I wanted to work "1FB9." The "1" indicated Central Division, "FB" indicated Foot Beat and the "9" meant the unit designation. 1FB9 was the area on Flower Street and Figueroa Street.

It included the high-rise buildings where all the pretty girls worked. It was the wealthiest part of downtown and was a great foot beat.

Carmella Ruzco and Pete Warten, a couple of young hot shots, had transferred to the division three months before us and locked up the assignment, even though we had seniority on them. The result was our assignment to 1FB1, which was not the most sought after beat in the city.

Almost immediately, six of the business owners met with us and complained about a dope dealer who was working the street in front of their businesses. The area in question covered two blocks on Main Street, between 3rd Street and 5th Street. The dealer seemed to prefer the east side of the street, but occasionally drifted to the other side.

He stashed his rock cocaine away from the street and only carried an amount for a single sale in his right hand. He accepted money in his left hand and released the narcotics from his right hand.

We observed his actions, but were never quite able to see the actual cocaine. There was no question in our mind he was selling dope. The only thing missing was our seeing it. Every time we closed in on him, he would throw his contraband into the busy street. The cars, trucks and city buses immediately destroyed it and ground it into the asphalt. We tried and tried to catch the suspect, but he always eluded us and remained a step ahead of us. We couldn't put a case together because it was just too difficult to get close to him without being spotted in our uniform.

The businessmen were really getting upset with our inability to clean up their area. We could tell this when the sergeant kept reminding us that the chief was tired of their calls and letters of complaint. Our job was to get the sergeant off our backs, which would get the chief off his back. This could only be accomplished by getting Rossmore out of our beat area. The courts were so lenient, they would do very little if we actually caught him. Randy told Rossmore on three different occasions to stop selling dope or move into another city.

Randy was really getting bugged by this guy. The suspect, Bobby Rossmore, was a dirty male, white, about thirty-five years old, five feet ten inches with long, stringy, dirty brown hair, beard and moustache. It seemed he always had a cigarette hanging between his lips and if he didn't, he probably had dope in his right hand.

Randy referred to him as "The Buzzard" because he preyed on the inept, the stupid, nonthinking people that were the victims of his scam. Every time we checked the suspect out, he was clean and just laughed at us. Randy didn't like this at all.

We worked diligently for about three weeks trying to get close to Rossmore. This effort was to no avail. Randy said, "We have got to devise a plan to end this."

We stopped at Clifford's Cafeteria for our sixth cup of morning coffee. This one was to plan our strategy. On the foot beat, we had to like coffee because the merchants were always asking us to come in for a cup. Police officers knew they really wanted cheap security, but we liked the free coffee!

The next day, Randy took me into one of the men's stores and worked a deal with the owner. The owner took the mannequin out of the window that had a large winter overcoat on it. Randy put the large coat on which completely covered his uniform and then stood in the window like a mannequin. I positioned myself in the front edge of the alley across the street slightly northwest of Randy's location. I was to be visible and a decoy.

While "The Buzzard" walked north on the east side of the street, he always kept one eye on me. He knew Randy and I were always together, but not today. Rossmore passed by Randy in the window never realizing Randy was the mannequin. Randy observed that the suspect's right fist was tight and knew it would be full of dope.

After Rossmore got about ten feet past the store, Randy quickly came out of the display window, threw off the coat, ran up behind him grabbing his right hand and kept it clinched. I just watched as Randy jaywalked Bobby to the alley. Known dope buyers clearly saw the grab by Randy and observed Rossmore being marched across the street. My job was to act nonchalantly about the entire event.

Our car was parked about fifty feet back in the alley in plain view. When we arrived at the rear of our car, Rossmore was asked to turn around so he would be facing back out to Main Street. He was looking back toward the street where the people who bought the dope could see him talking with us. No handcuffs were placed on Rossmore and we gave him a lot of space. Naturally he wouldn't run. We just talked politely and calmly to him.

Soon Rossmore said we had better take him to the station and book him. He also added that he knew he would be on the street again within an hour. He was right if we booked him, but this was not in the plan.

Although Randy and I didn't smoke, we had a pack of cigarettes to offer Rossmore. He naturally took it and we lit one for him. Anyone looking down the alley would think that Rossmore was our good ole buddy, or a good informant. Randy dropped the handful of rock cocaine to the asphalt. Rossmore said, "You have to book the dope as evidence." With that, Randy placed his size-twelve army boot on top of the dope and ground it into the asphalt. He ground it up just as the vehicles had done when it was thrown into the street by Bobby.

Randy said, "When you walk out of this alley, if you deal dope anymore, your life is not going to be worth much of anything."

Rossmore retorted, "Are you going to shoot me if you see me on your beat again? Give me a break." With that he began laughing.

We laughed with him and Randy said, "No, we are not going to shoot you. That would be illegal, however, everyone into dope on this beat knows we caught you. The word will be out that we ground up your dope in the asphalt and gave you cigarettes. They will know we even lit one for you and that we talked for a short time."

I concluded with, "Bobby, tomorrow, we are going to put it on the street that we didn't book you because you gave us good information for better arrests. You are now going to be known as an 'informant.' You will be dead meat on the streets of L.A. with the dope dealers and buyers. I suggest you leave town. The decision is yours."

We got in our car and drove away to the other end of our beat. Rossmore was left in the alley no longer laughing as before, but rather asking us to please book him.

We assumed Bobby Rossmore left Los Angeles because we never saw him again.

The merchants were as happy as could be. More importantly, the sergeant was now off our back and the chief was satisfied. Believe it or not, after the Bobby Rossmore problem solution, we went six months without Sergeant Gomez's getting in our face over more productivity. The chief received about a dozen commendatory letters from the merchants, which made everyone happy.

Everything was great until Sergeant Gomez retired six months later. Then we got a newly appointed young sergeant by the name of Danny Wolfer. He had just been transferred into the division. He had a five-digit serial number, which meant he had less than ten years on the job. Sergeant Wolfer knew more than anyone about everything, especially about policing the city and he didn't mind telling you so. He never listened when you talked to him. He just liked to hear himself talk.

Randy could not stand this guy. He never was insubordinate, but the chemistry just wasn't there between these two. I learned to tolerate Wolfer.

One hot Wednesday afternoon, Sergeant Wolfer broadcast over the radio frequency, "1FB1, 1FB1. Meet the supervisor on the northeast corner of Pershing Square, Code Two." Code Two meant that the call was urgent and should be handled without delay. To an officer in a black and white police vehicle, it simply meant "hurry," but no red emergency lights or siren was authorized on the call.

What a guy. All he had to do was request our location on the radio and meet us there as we were on foot, or he could drive down Main Street and Hill Street between 1st Street and 10th Street and he would have found us. Instead, he had the communication operator give us a call to meet him, Code 2.

We wondered if the new sergeant thought we were going to run from 10th and Main, to 5th and Hill to meet him. An experienced sergeant would never have taken this approach, but he would learn.

Randy "rogered" the call, gave our location and quoted a forty-five-minute delay due to our distance. Sure enough, Wolfer said to stand by our location and he would meet us. I bet he never asked a foot beat officer to meet him, Code Two, again! Randy just laughed, that is before the sergeant arrived. Then we both put on our hard-working business faces until he left.

The important subject the sergeant had to discuss with us was pedestrian citations. He informed us that the chief was concerned about pedestrians being involved in traffic accidents by crossing against the Don't Walk signal or jaywalking mid-block.

In California, due to the large number of vehicles that are registered and the need to control their activity, the legislature enacted a vehicle code. The vehicle code not only regulated the activities of the drivers, but it controlled the activities of the pedestrians. We knew the law was strict.

We explained to the sergeant that during the last twelve months there had not been a single traffic accident involving a pedestrian on our beat. Sergeant Wolfer would not budge so we said we would clean up our beat. He said he would be monitoring our progress.

Randy said Wolfer wanted to generate more revenue for the city. I argued that his motivation was to get the lieutenant off his back. He said civil liability in the civil suits was probably getting the insurance companies upset and they were the ones probably putting the heat on the chief of police. Either way, Randy insisted money was the motivating factor to send Wolfer to our beat.

Then we returned to Clifford's Cafeteria for another cup of coffee to devise another plan for getting the sergeant off our backs. We liked to be left alone.

During the next ten working days, we cited ten people each day. Randy wrote five tickets and I wrote five tickets, but the way we wrote the tickets was unique.

We went to each major intersection on the beat and during a fifteen-minute period, stopped a group of from five to ten people who jaywalked or walked against the Don't Walk signal. We led them to the sidewalk and admonished the group in a funny way. We told them we could cite everyone or let them flip coins to see who would be cited. We also suggested that the others not cited could chip in and help pay the ticket of the one who received the ticket.

Randy and I also asked the pedestrians to pass the word that henceforth, everyone would be cited if they stepped off the curb before the Walk signal or after the Don't Walk signal started to flash, or if they illegally jaywalked. We requested their help and they did get the word out. Everyone liked us and felt we were their cops.

One thing for sure, no one on our beat would step off the curb in violation of the vehicle code. At least they would not do it if there was a cop within two blocks. The word was out and they stood on the sidewalks like tin soldiers. It was unbelievable. No more violations, at least while we were around.

At the end of the ten day period Randy and I had written one hundred moving tickets to pedestrians. On the eleventh working day, we put out a call to Sergeant Wolfer. "1L30, 1L30, meet the officers,

1FB1 at 10th and Main Street, southeast corner. The call is Code Two."

"1L30" was the radio call sign for our sergeant and the 1FB1 was our foot beat designation. I told Randy he was pushing his luck with the sergeant, but he just couldn't resist and laughed. It was funny.

Wolfer immediately "rogered" the call, sped to our location and jumped out like Johnny on the Spot. Then Randy told him, "Sarge, we have a problem."

Of course Wolfer bit the hook and replied, "What's wrong, can I help? Do we need more units?"

Randy continued, "Sarge, we have worked our tail off during the last couple of weeks writing the pedestrians as you directed. We have written at least a hundred citations and we just can't find anymore violators. Would it be possible for you to help us? We would like to write more tickets."

Randy sounded like a sixth grader asking permission to go to the restroom. I nearly split a gut, but didn't crack a smile until Wolfer left our location. Wolfer wasn't sure, but I think he suspected that he had been had, although Randy looked so serious.

One day we were walking near 4th and Hill and I saw smoke coming from the second story of a dental office. Smoke was pouring out of the window so I keyed my portable radio and requested fire department units to respond Code 3 to the fire. Randy and I ran into the building. He evacuated the first floor and I handled the top floor. The last tenant on the second floor was Dr. Kendall Parnicci, a dentist.

I yelled at him that we were evacuating the building due to a fire. He kept delaying his exit as he was grabbing up things to take out of the building. I entered the hallway and saw an elderly man in a wheelchair rolling slowly toward the elevator which was not working by now. He obviously didn't hear very well so I picked him up and carried him down the flight of stairs. He only weighed about a hundred and thirty pounds so I put him over my shoulder like a sack of fertilizer and down we went. I gently set him on the sidewalk in a shady spot and leaned him up against the building a couple of doors down, south of the burning building, out of harm's way.

I spent just a few seconds consoling and reassuring him and then immediately ran back into the burning building to retrieve his wheelchair from the second floor. When I returned to the man's location I carefully sat him in the wheelchair and made sure he was comfortable and okay. Even though he was not very articulate, it was obvious he appreciated my help. I didn't want to cut the man short as he thanked me and shook my hand. I had to check the second floor again as I kept thinking of the dentist who had not yet exited the burning building.

When I reached the top of the stairway for the third time, I was getting a little winded. Dr. Parnicci was still not coming and I had not seen him. I went into his office and finally found the dentist back in a small room near the rear of the complex. I yelled to him, "Doc, what's the delay?"

He mumbled something but I didn't understand.

I got closer and said, "Can I help you?"

The doctor answered, "No, it's not necessary. I've got it."

I replied, "What have you got?"

He responded, "These records."

He had loaded three boxes about the size of copy paper onto a small dolly and he insisted on taking the boxes. I helped the doctor with the boxes on the small dolly.

As we got near the stairway I asked him, "Doc, are these your patient's dental records?"

He looked at me, pushed his thick bifocals back on his nose, looked me directly in the eye and replied, "Heck no, these are my accounts receivable. Let the dental records burn!"

At this point I cracked up. The last person I was to save in this fire taught me a lesson about dental offices. I learned what the most important thing is to a dentist.

Randy got a good chuckle out of the accounts receivable story. He said the love of money is the root of all evil but I knew he hadn't come up with that. He had heard Lieutenant Allen say that in a roll call a few days earlier.

After the fire department finally arrived at the scene they put out the fire relatively quickly. Luckily, no one was hurt. The building owner suffered about three hundred thousand dollars in his monetary loss. Sergeant Wolfer liked the action that Randy and I took at the burning building so he naturally wrote both of us a commendation letter for our quick thinking and action.

We were good for another six months then a problem started to show up on the divisional pin maps in the Jewelry Mart. These businesses were located mainly on Hill Street between 5th and 7th streets.

Routinely, Randy and I checked the crime reports for our beat. We started to see a pattern of distraction-type thefts with considerable losses. On most of the crimes the suspects were described as males from South America. They appeared to be very organized and did not mind showing their faces. Their identification was not of concern to them.

We established a plan to work on eliminating these thefts, naturally with Sergeant Wolfer's input. We staked out on jewelry sales people's cars then followed them in an unmarked police car. With Wolfer's approval, we slipped out of our uniforms into plain clothes on selected occasions.

After working the situation for about two months we made thirteen felony arrests. We were now able to track an organization that worked on distraction thefts.

The bandits would identify a particular jewelry salesperson and watch their every move for several days. When the suspects were ready to make their move, they would stick an ice pick in a tire or the radiator of the jeweler's car, which would cause a slow leak.

The victim would leave the Jewelry Mart area putting their briefcase filled with jewels on the back seat and drive onto the freeway. Ten minutes later their tire or radiator would disable the car and they would pull to the right side of the freeway to check it out.

Then a good Samaritan, so the victim thought, would stop to help. One suspect helped take off the tire or check the radiator while the victim was distracted and his attention was not on the jewelry.

The second suspect went into the back seat and picked-up the victim's briefcase or other containers carrying the jewelry. The suspect took it back to his car and then the two suspects simply got in their car and drove away. The victim never knew what was happening until it was too late.

The suspects were smooth and organized. They were bold and brazen and stalked their prey for a long time before they moved in, but when they made their move, it was a large theft.

Later, we discovered they would take a group of three or four thieves and drive up to a clothing store. They would boldly walk in and grab two or three racks of clothing, exit the store, throw the merchandise into the trunk and back seat of the car and drive away. We followed them on a couple of occasions and discovered they were taking the items to a rental storage locker. We found evidence they were then shipping the merchandise back to Colombia where most of the suspects were from.

As the origin of these organized bandits was Colombia, we called them the "Colombians." Sergeant Wolfer insisted that we refer to the group as the "South American Organized Crime Group." He said it sounded better not to identify any one by nationality. He said it was politically incorrect to do so.

As a result of our good work, the captain lent Sergeant Wolfer, Randy and me to the Burglary-Auto Division, B.A.D., for three months. The chief had formed a task force in B.A.D. to combat the distraction-theft problem.

Randy and I figured the chief had probably received a lot of telephone calls and letters from the business owners in the Jewelry Mart complaining about the large losses in the recent crime sprees. That's the way it worked. The squeaky wheel always gets the oil.

The LAPD loan program is a "flim-flam" way for management to look us over in a prestigious job such as B.A.D. Neither of us wanted to keep working the detective job. Randy kept saying he wanted to get back to the beat. I thought he meant 1FB1, the Main and Hill Street beat, but he finally dropped it on me.

Carmella and Pete, the officers assigned to 1FB9, had been accepted to Metro. Metropolitan Division was a good place to work. They worked in uniform and were assigned an unmarked police vehicle. Also, they were permitted to use the car to drive to and from work.

Everyone knew we were not permitted to use the police vehicle for personal business, but some with a take-home car, from the chiefs down to the Metro cop, occasionally used the car for transportation other than work. If they got in a traffic accident during unauthorized use of the vehicles, the driver was always "just going to stop by the station." The Mayor never figured it out. Or, maybe he did!

Now Carmella and Pete were going to join the Metro elite. This meant 1FB9 would be open on the next transfer and we wanted it.

Armed with this knowledge, Randy and I went to discuss the matter with the day watch commander. He just happened to be Randy's classmate at the academy but he had progressed up the organizational ladder several steps. Randy did the talking. He requested that we be returned to our division from our loan to B.A.D. and assigned to 1FB9, the premier foot beat. The lieutenant said he would do everything he could to effect this.

Sergeant Wolfer pleaded with us to stay in B.A.D., but we graciously declined. Wolfer got transferred into the division permanently and he assured us that he would have us transferred in on the first two openings in the division.

Randy said the sergeant just wanted us to carry him, as he didn't know anything about street police work. He insisted we were Wolfer's ticket to success and for him to make lieutenant. But Randy still didn't trust the sergeant, so I took what he said with a grain of salt.

During the three-month loan, my blue uniform shrank. There was no question in my mind why the detectives on the third floor of Parker Center put on so much weight. The job requires too much sitting in the office and not enough moving around. So to the Academy I went to buy three new uniforms and start my work-out program again. The cost of the new uniform's was quite a penalty to pay for a three-month loan that I really didn't like.

We got the beat assignment as the watch commander, Randy's buddy, had promised. We walked and looked and looked at this new beat. There were not nearly the crime problems here that we had experienced on 1FB1, which included Main Street and Hill Street. Everyone here seemed to be much better off financially.

Randy thought we got the assignment because of his contact with the lieutenant. I didn't have the heart to tell Randy that the lieutenant and I had met in the coffee room at Parker Center about two weeks before Randy asked the lieutenant for the job. When I ran into him, I was sipping on a cup of coffee and reading my Aircraft Owner's and Pilots Association Magazines. He walked over to me and started talking about flying. Come to find out, the lieutenant was a private pilot also and had logged about 400 hours in his own Cessna-172. We talked about planes for at least an hour before we finally left the coffee room. I think the lieutenant liked airplanes and then realized how worthy and well qualified we were for the assignment! I just couldn't pop Randy's balloon.

On December 28, the Monday after Christmas, we had a day to remember. There were a lot of shoppers and anxious people on the streets today. At the end of the day, Randy and I were not sure if we had made the right decision to give up our loan to B.A.D.

Shortly after 4:30 p.m., just before going end-of-watch, we were walking northbound on Figueroa, on the east side of the street, approaching 8th Street. We were headed for our police vehicle when a call came out, "1A97, 1A97, a disturbance by a man in the law office, 778 South Figueroa, Room 4801. Handle your call Code 2."

1A97, a Central Division two-officer black and white police unit was getting ready to also go end-of-watch.

They didn't want the call, so they broadcast, "1A97, Roger on the call, but we quote a twenty-minute delay due to distance and traffic."

That sounded similar to the response I gave communications when I was assigned the Wade Gun Store Caper many years earlier. As we were about one hundred feet from the front door of the building, the fact that Randy said he needed the overtime money and the fact that very few 415, disturbance calls, require paperwork, we keyed our radio and said, "1FB9, we will handle the disturbance at 778 South Figueroa Street. We are at the location. Cancel for 1A97."

1A97 switched to the tactical frequency and said, "1FB9, thanks much. We owe you one."

Room 4801 was probably on the forty-eighth floor of the ultramodern skyscraper. We knew a little bit about the building as several movies had been filmed there since we were assigned to the beat. We had done some P.R. for the department while they were making the movies.

The mayor had called the chief and asked that we handle crowd control. The public relations were easy and just another part of the job.

Randy had met a girl who worked in the building and occasionally stopped in to see her. Her office was in room thirty-four something and was logically located on the thirty-fourth floor. Room 4801 had to be near the top of the fifty-story building.

One problem with the building was that in certain portions of the structure our police radios did not receive or transmit. It was known as a "dead spot" by communication experts. The remedy was to erect another large relay antenna on one of the surrounding buildings which cost the city another twenty-five to thirty grand. Only the police union pushed for such expenditures and this was not their most important issue on December 28 or before.

Up the elevator we went to the twenty-fifth floor. Then we changed to another elevator that serviced the twenty-sixth to fiftieth floors. Randy didn't like the tall buildings. He always said he felt that the building was swaying with the wind, but he concealed his feelings when others were in the elevator.

We got off on the forty-eighth floor. Room 4801 was just to the left as we got off the elevator. The office sign said, "Law Offices of Bradmoor, Johnson, Solomon and Associates."

We entered the office and to our surprise there was no one in the reception area, but we heard people talking loudly in what appeared to be the conference room located toward the center portion of the floor, away from the offices with the panoramic views of the downtown skyline. It was now shortly after 4:40 p. m. and Randy was about to earn the overtime he thought he wanted.

We walked back into the conference room as though we had been invited. Seated on one side of the long conference table was a young man who I estimated as age thirty-something. My first impression of him could be summed up as a jerk. We identified him as a client. The older, well-dressed man we assumed was his attorney.

On the opposite side of the table was a woman, apparently the wife who had filed for divorce. Next to her sat her attorney. There was a good-looking, middle-aged secretary sitting near the door at the far end of the table. Later, we learned that she was the smart one who called the police before the matter escalated to the point where no one would be able to call for help.

As we walked in, the man who now became the suspect, said, "Come on in and sit down, officers. I'm James North and I'm getting the short end of this divorce."

I responded with, "Thank you, Mr. North, but what is the police problem?"

He replied, "Officer, there is no problem, if you cooperate." Then he placed his right hand on the table and said, "This is a hand grenade. I have removed the pin. I have six sticks of dynamite in my briefcase."

He opened the briefcase and showed us the six sticks of dynamite, which appeared to be attached to a percussion-type detonator like those I had seen when I was in the Army.

North continued with, "I intend to blow up this woman and her attorney. You two cops, my attorney and this secretary will be joining us, if you don't do exactly as I say. Sit down and keep your hands on the table!"

Now there were seven seated at the table. The suspect looked a lot like the drug dealer Bobby Rossmore. This guy, James North, was a man totally flipped out over his impending divorce and financial disaster that would follow. All of this was probably over money. Both the plaintiff and the defendant in this case acted like real losers. At this point, it was hard to determine who would be the winner when it was all over.

Just as we got seated, with our hands in plain view on the table clearly away from our guns, the building began to sway and shake. We weren't sure but figured we were experiencing a strong earthquake.

The lights and power went out and there was total darkness in the room. Ceiling tiles fell to the floor and a couple of them hit the table. Several chairs rolled to the other side of the room. We could hear glass breaking.

The emergency generators for the top five floors and the stairwell of the entire building had failed. There was still no power and our suspect was in command with a hand grenade in his hand and six sticks of dynamite in his briefcase.

I knew I had seen the hand grenade and I assumed Randy had seen it. There was little doubt in my mind about the dynamite in the briefcase being real. There was no room to take a chance. North and the earthquake were in control.

North began yelling and screaming for no one to move. Then I interjected, "James, let's all just be calm and quiet. No one is going to do anything until you okay it. Everyone just sit still. James is in control. Let's keep calm and let James tell us what he wants us to do."

At that moment, there was a very strong aftershock. This brought down more of the ceiling tiles and caused more glass to shatter. Pictures and plaques fell off the wall. One of the tiles hit the secretary and caused a slight injury to her face. Shattered glass cut one of the attorney's hands as well as the suspect's arm. Fortunately, no one was seriously injured.

The sound of the breaking glass in the dark caused a very eerie feeling as we had no idea where it was. No one moved for fear of stepping on it. We were still in total darkness.

Randy and I should have brought our flashlights but they were down in the police car. We could sure use one of them now!

I could not see anything but I was sure Randy felt sick and wished we had let 1A97 handle their own call. The overtime was not going to be worth it today and there would be a lot of paperwork.

It was obvious that our weapons and marksmanship were not the solution to this mess. We were afraid to even think about removing our hands from the table in fear the lights might come back on and James would flip out and turn loose the grenade.

Then I said, "Doesn't everyone agree that Mr. North is in complete control and we all are going to do exactly as he says. Right?"

About that time, we felt another strong aftershock and then the answers to my question started coming in like an old-fashioned revival. Even Randy was a believer as we sat there in the dark feeling a little helpless. Which was worse, the crazy man with the grenade and dynamite or the strong earthquake? We were at their mercy.

Had Marie been here, she would have shaken her finger at me and lectured me on the fact that this was one of those circumstances in which all of the money in the world wouldn't buy your way out of this mess. It was crazy!

I felt the best tactic at this point was to keep North, as well as everyone else, calm and buy time while we waited for at least some light.

I kneed Randy and then said to the group, "James, you are in control, but may I make a suggestion?"

We let North ramble on for six or seven minutes. He said Jennifer's attorney had brought documents to the meeting that would ruin him for life. We figured he was high on speed or some other drug. *Just let him work it out without blowing us up.* Jennifer's attorney had let everyone go early when the disturbance with North began. At least we knew there were no other employees remaining in the office.

North's tone of voice had changed as though he was shaken by the earthquake. Finally he said, "What is your suggestion?"

I thought he had forgotten about my suggestion. At least he had some reasoning ability.

I replied, "I recommend you hold on to the grenade really tight. Then you could have all of us line up where I lead the line with you at the rear of the line. Everyone could place their right hand on the person's shoulder in front of them. I could try to find our way out of this room so we can get some light. That way you can see that we are complying with your wishes. Be assured no one will challenge your authority. You are in command and we recognize it."

With this, Randy kneed me, which I interpreted to mean he agreed. Two or three of the others chimed in with their vocal support of the recommendation.

I asked North, "Do you want to try it?"

There was a long pause. Then he said, "The first one to screw up will be responsible for causing the death of everyone here. I mean it. I'll blow all of us up. I have nothing to live for any more."

In my command voice I came back with, "Everyone stand up very slowly and I am going to work my way around the table to those on the left side of the table from where I'm sitting. Is that okay, James?"

James said, "Yeah, but you had better move slowly and you had better not double cross me."

I said, "James, my name is Brad and my partner's name is Randy. Why don't you tell me where you want Randy in our line. Do you want him behind me?"

North respond with, "No, I want you first, followed by my attorney, then Jennifer's attorney, then Jennifer, then the secretary, then your buddy Randy and I will follow him. If you screw up, your buddy will be the first to feel the blast. Don't double cross me."

Just as I got up, there was another strong aftershock. I stumbled and bumped the table. This time lights hanging on the ceiling fell and narrowly missed several of us. Furniture moved around in the room and books fell off the shelves. The thought came to mind, I would have been halfway home by now if we had not taken 1A97's radio call. This kind of overtime was definitely not worth it.

I talked calmly as I slowly and very cautiously worked my way around to my left and finally reached the area of Jennifer and her attorney. I quietly lined them up and instructed them to place their right hand on the person's shoulder in front of them.

Everyone was a little apprehensive wondering when the next jolt would occur. I got the entire line in order like the game "pin the tail on the donkey." We couldn't see our hands in front of our faces. It was the blind leading the blind.

Then North spoke up telling Randy to carry the briefcase in his left hand. I knew Randy wished we had passed on the call, but he said he was complying with North's instruction.

What I didn't know was that Randy picked up the briefcase, but as he passed around the table his leg touched Jennifer's attorney's briefcase. Randy was cool. He picked up this case and slipped James' briefcase under the table.

Randy then shifted the briefcase into his left hand so North and everyone else would think he was complying with the instruction. Finally, he placed his right hand on the right shoulder of the secretary just as he had been ordered. North touched the table to work his way around the table before he placed his right hand on Randy's shoulder.

I would have given anything to have had a photo of this ordeal. I could just imagine Randy in roll call telling the guys about how Brad led the blind to see the light. They would double over laughing and I would have to take it.

Jennifer's attorney gave us directions to find the hallway, which was also very dark. With the clocks turned back to standard time, it had to be dark outside by now. Later we found out that all of the power in downtown was out. This added to the darkness in the hallways.

As we shuffled along like kids in a game, North brought up the rear. We went slowly and I tried to keep James talking. I would ask him before taking any action, hoping to give him a feeling of security and letting him know he was in control.

When we arrived at the open reception area, it was also dark. I thought we would reach the glassed area and lights would be shining, but everything was dark. As we looked out at the city, we could see many fires burning.

After a few more steps there was a suction force from the area near the windows. I realized that at least five or six of the large windows on the south side of the building had been knocked out due to the earthquake.

The wind blowing pulled us toward the windows so we didn't want to get too close. As we entered the open area, Randy suddenly dropped the briefcase and turned and grabbed James' left hand, making it tight as a baseball pitcher, as he pushed him near the open window.

All I could think about was the dynamite in the briefcase. I wasn't about to open the case and check it so I grabbed it and threw it out the open window. By now Randy had knocked North to the floor, but he wouldn't budge on his grip on the suspect's left hand.

The last time I saw Randy's big Irish hands on someone else's fist was when he grabbed Bobby Rossmore when he was holding rock cocaine, but this time Randy had the most intense look on his face that I had ever seen.

I ran to Randy's rescue and yelled to the others to move back. We cuffed James' right wrist to the door knob with my handcuffs, kicked him in the groin so he fell limp to the floor, but Randy would not let go of his left hand. Finally, we got the secretary to get us three heavy-duty paper clips. We opened them up into a straight line, carefully threaded the clips into the hand grenade then bent them back hoping they would hold the handle in the position to prevent activation.

When Randy carefully let go of his left hand, the three large paper clips worked just like the original cotter key. We set the grenade on the opened top drawer of the receptionist's desk. Then we uncuffed

North from the door knob and cuffed his two hands behind his back and under his belt to further restrain him.

Randy quietly told me that Jennifer's attorney's briefcase was the one I threw out the open window. He said the briefcase with the dynamite was under the conference table in the other room. I realized I had just destroyed the briefcase and all the evidence that would have made Jennifer's case against James.

Oh well. What mattered was that we were alive and no one was blown up. Now our attention had to be on getting the seven of us down the forty-eight floors.

Under normal circumstances we would notify the bomb squad to handle the situation, but the telephones were out of service, our radios were not working and due to the earthquake, certainly the bomb squad would have much higher priorities.

Randy and I decided to leave the briefcase with the dynamite under the conference table with notes attached to the conference room door, briefcase and on the table that said:

CAUTION-Dynamite in the Briefcase-CAUTION
DO NOT TOUCH
Contact
Phillips or O'Rilley
Central Division
LAPD

Then we debated whether we should carry the hand grenade down the forty-eight floors or leave it in another office. We finally agreed to leave it in one of the law partner's offices in his top drawer with similar signs on the door, top of desk and drawer.

Randy said by putting it in the law partner's office, if it should go off, it would create upward mobility for some young lawyer. He had gone through a divorce a couple years earlier and had no use for attorneys.

I escorted North, who had a headache and a sore groin, as we started down the stair well.

Many times during my career, I had gone down the eight flights of stairs at Parker Center, but the forty-eight floors in this law building were something else. It took a long time as we took one step at a time feeling each one with our toes. We held tightly to the rail with our left hand. We had to make at least three stops for our group to rest.

We did not run into or hear another person going down the stairway. Everyone else must have evacuated the building at least a half-hour ahead of us. The earthquake had forced people to move quickly.

We constantly tried our radios to put out a call for assistance, but they didn't work. We were in a "dead spot" or LAPD Communication was out due to the earthquake. We tried the telephone in the law office, the pay phone in the lobby and the security phones in the lobby. All were not working. So we headed for the station.

As a result of the earthquake, about five hundred million dollars worth of damage was done. The epicenter was on the east side of town. The quake registered 7.4. Eight freeway overpasses collapsed, several buckled and caved in, and massive structural damages resulted in eleven deaths and about three hundred reported injuries. All this took place while we handled our radio call.

When we finally got back to the station around 9:00 p.m., our lieutenant was still on duty. This was Randy's classmate. It was his buddy.

When he saw us walking in with an arrestee, we thought he was going to flip out. We could read it all over his face.

His first words were something like, "Where have you been? Why didn't you check in? Why were you making an arrest when the city was in a disaster mode?"

After listening to him rant for about five minutes, Randy got in his face, but wasn't quite insubordinate.

Randy leaned over the lieutenant; his face was red and the blood veins on Randy's face and forehead were ready to pop as he moved within one inch of his superior's face. Randy gritted his teeth as he informed him, in a low tone of voice, barely audible, the facts of the matter. Then the lieutenant understood.

Randy concluded with, "There are still six sticks of dynamite and one hand grenade on the forty-eighth floor."

After we left the lieutenant's office, Randy shook his head and said, "I wish we had brought the hand grenade and given it to the lieutenant."

9

THE VICE

Every couple of years the department sent officers to advanced officers training at the Police Academy. During the five-day course, officers reviewed newly enacted laws, CPR certification and departmental changes. As is often the case, civil liability was the driving force for the training. Liability considerations alone could justify the use of such a large amount of personnel resources.

For the cops, it was "R & R," recreation and relaxation; virtually a week's vacation. It was a good place to get the hot gossip from other cops. We kept up with the latest rumors and dirt in the department. We got a lot of useful and helpful information.

Lieutenant Mark Allen was one of the instructors on the third day. He taught a class on "Planning for Retirement." Although he was not assigned to Personnel Division, Allen was recognized as the department's retirement expert. He had all the institutional knowledge and knew how to make the system work.

His two-hour block of instruction was provided for all officers with at least ten years' service on the job. The department decided to provide this class because so many cops were not prepared for retirement, financially or emotionally.

Mark talked about when to retire in order to benefit from higher base pay, pay raises and cost-of-living adjustment on pensions. It could also affect tax benefits. He also told us how to cash out our sick time or use it at time of retirement.

All of this had to do with the date of appointment and which retirement plan we were hired under. It was very technical for street cops, but Mark made it simple.

His class was interesting and got a lot of good participation from the members. Everyone always gave him high evaluations, which justified his getting a two-hour class instead of the standard one-hour session.

After class, the lieutenant surprised me by asking if I wanted to get a burger at the Academy Restaurant. During lunch, we discussed a number of police subjects and small talk including family matters.

He mentioned that he had been transferred to Harbor Vice three months earlier.

Later, Allen tipped me off that on Friday a job announcement would be coming out for a vacant position in Harbor Vice. He said I should consider applying for the position. They would be looking for a mature, experienced officer who could work gambling, bookmakers, prostitutes and ABC violations.

I told the lieutenant I was three hundred nineteen on the new sergeant's list, but I had little chance to make it off this list. My chances were much better in winning the California Lottery than making sergeant this time.

Then Allen said, "Bradley, working vice is like getting your ticket punched for making sergeant. It gives you a tremendous experience that you can talk about at your next sergeant's oral interview. Brad, the LAPD needs undercover vice cops with integrity. You really ought to apply."

He was careful never to say I had the job if I wanted it. He just concluded with, "Bradley...Brad, you really ought to apply!" The use of my first name by a lieutenant was a clue as to my good standing and chances for getting the position.

So on Friday, after the announcement came out, I applied. Can you believe it? After I filed an application and had an oral interview, Captain Tom Powers and Lieutenant Allen selected me for the job over thirty-eight other candidates.

While walking the beat on our last work day before I was transferred, Randy told me Allen wanted me because of my loyalty. Randy insisted that I was not cut out for vice because I had flat feet from walking the beat with him!

I defended my Vice selection by telling Randy that the lieutenant respected me for not taking my tax-free pension when I was shot in Griffith Park years before. I was working for the lieutenant in Central Division when I got shot. Then I threw in the fact that I was the best qualified for the assignment.

I hated leaving Randy on the foot beat but we knew he was not going anywhere. He would be spending the next six years, until he planned to retired, looking at the pretty girls on the beat.

Randy was satisfied staying where he was. He didn't want to be transferred or even promoted. He was single for the second time and just wanted the sergeant to leave him alone. He didn't like being supervised.

The first night I drove to Harbor Station from my home, I thought I had signed up for "freeway therapy." I was assigned to the night watch and worked from 4:30 p.m. until 1:00 a.m, but we could have all the overtime we wanted. Regardless, it was still a thirty-eight-mile drive each way. I had forgotten how close Parker Center was to my home compared to Harbor Station.

Vice crimes are often called victimless crimes, but they're not. The pain and suffering that are caused in society because of these crimes is difficult to measure. Families are torn apart but the vice cop's mission is to somewhat control the activity.

Most police departments have procedures that require enforcement action when vice activity is complained of, conspicuous or commercialized. LAPD was no exception and we called them the three "C's."

I floundered for about two weeks and then Lieutenant Allen sent me to the Vice School at the academy. This one-week training was intense, detailed and informative and I'm sure helped to reduce the city's liability.

While at the Vice School, I learned from the informal chatter that Lieutenant Allen was on the captain's list and would be getting promoted within the next two years. He had finished number four on the list. It was interesting to find out Allen had made sergeant in the minimum time of three and a half years and then made lieutenant in just two years. The brass made him stay as a lieutenant for twelve years before they let him out of the doghouse.

Word among the rank and file was the brass was very jealous of Allen. He was well-liked, a college graduate, went back to school and obtained a law degree and passed the bar. That is enough to justify envy. Mark and his wife were so sharp they formed a small business and published "How-to-Do" books. His books were on subjects such as how to get hired as a cop, how to get promoted and his latest book was on life after the LAPD.

Mark Allen was a real threat to insecure police administrators. He was very bright, but the greatest threat was being well liked by the troops. He would have been elected chief by the troops if it were an elected position.

Upon my return to Harbor Station, I was assigned to work a massage parlor known for prostitution and permit violations. The parlor was located on PCR, Pacific Coast Road, just west of 24th Street.

There were a number of local business owners and residents who had complained about this establishment. There was also an elementary school nearby. Harbor Vice had been unsuccessful in making solid arrests or closing the doors of the business for over a two-year period.

My partner was Debbie Ramsey. She had only five years on the job, but she had been in Vice for the last four months and it showed by her in-depth knowledge. Debbie was sharp and witty. She was number forty-three on the sergeant's list and would be promoted in about eight months.

We sat in the coffee room and put together a plan. I was going to be the operator and she was going to be my backup. She would tape my conversation with the prostitute who acted as a masseuse.

At 8:10 p.m. I entered the massage parlor and asked the receptionist if it would be possible to get a massage. She directed me to Room 3. I was provided with a robe and towel as she left the room.

I stripped to my shorts and put the robe on. I folded my clothes neatly and placed them on the chair. My miniature microphone was in my right shoe, which was under the chair. The microphone would transmit to Debbie and her tape recorder, which she had turned on. She waited inside our unmarked police car directly across the street from the parlor. On my verbal cue of "goldmine," Debbie would quickly enter the business and assist me in making the arrest.

I missed having my badge, gun and handcuffs in the room, but this was the only way we could make the bust. I set on the edge of the massage table. Street cops didn't like to do their work without their police equipment. It was a very insecure feeling.

It didn't feel as if I was making a routine arrest. It was different. I felt more like I was in the doctor's office waiting to take my annual physical. The next thing heard might be "Turn your head and cough."

Soon a beautiful twenty-something Japanese girl entered the room. She spoke very broken English with a definite Japanese accent. SuLin made some small talk then told me to take off the robe. I untied it, but left it on.

She now could see my right stomach area. Her eyes honed in on my old gunshot wounds. In a suspicious inflection in her voice she said, "What is this?"

I shuttered and replied, "U. S. Navy, Operation Desert Storm!"

She asked, "Oh? How?"

"Um, um. Yes, I brave Navy man."

SuLin replied, "Okay. Okay. You now lie down flat on stomach on table."

I complied, but kept the robe on.

Suddenly, she asked me what kind of work I did. Off the top of my head, I told her I was in the Navy stationed in Long Beach. Then she threw me for a loop.

She said, "What ship are you stationed on?"

I was completely thrown off guard. I couldn't think of the name of a Navy ship except for the *USS Arizona*.

I responded with a couple of coughs and finally stuttered, "I'm assigned to the *USS Arizona*."

Then I nearly split a gut when I realized that the Japanese had sunk the ship in Pearl Harbor on December 7, 1941, a day President Roosevelt said would be a day that would live in our memory forever. I was glad that SuLin did not know U. S. or Japanese military history.

SuLin answered, "Oh!" and stared to rub my legs under the robe. Then she started moving her hands up my leg to my groin area. I immediately puckered up as I thought about my *Arizona* answer.

Debbie had to be cracking up laughing when she heard me say I was assigned to the *USS Arizona*. I thought the arrest was blown at that point, but it wasn't. My problem would be the ribbing I'd get from Debbie and the other vice cops. They would never let me live this one down.

For the next five minutes SuLin kept feeling around and rubbing my body below the waist. Then she popped the questions with the usual word game.

"You like loving, yes? You want good loving? I love you all night."

Then we exchanged definitions and terms so I could get her to specifically state what she would do sexually. Finally she said she would do a good job for fifty dollars.

I was quickly learning from first-hand experience not by reading books, how to be a vice cop. I knew Debbie was thoroughly enjoying my role playing and so I kept it up. We yakked for about ten more minutes on what and how she was going to do and for how much.

Debbie was waiting for my signal. I tried to get SuLin to agree to forty dollars. The idea upset and irritated SuLin.

With that, I jumped up, tied the knot on my robe and shouted, "Goldmine," which was the signal for Debbie to come in.

SuLin thought I said, "Gold digger!"

She began yelling, "I no gold digger. I no gold digger. I give you good sex and lovin' for your money. I no gold digger."

She started to hit me repeatedly on the back and head. It didn't really hurt. It was just funny, but SuLin was mad.

Debbie intentionally stalled for about two minutes before she slowly walked in, identified herself and put the handcuffs on SuLin. My partner looked at me and smiled with, "Brad, you insulted the lady. You really shouldn't be so cheap when doing business with a woman!"

I retorted, "Would you please take SuLin out so I can get dressed!"

All the elements of the crime were clearly recorded on the tape and it made a good case. The arrest held up. Four months later, SuLin's visa was terminated and she was returned to Japan.

However, the defense attorney was successful in obtaining three continuances for their hearing before the Police Commission. This gave the massage parlor another ten months of doing business before their hearing.

At the public hearing, the local business owners and residents spoke out emphatically about their opposition to the business. The Police Commission revoked the operating permits and the massage parlor went out of business. Debbie said they would probably go somewhere else and open up. They would do it under a different business name and owner on the Police Commission permit request. She said it had happened on more than one occasion.

The department had a strict policy that prohibited an officer from working vice for more than eighteen months. It was a good rule because after a period of time the officer got burned out.

Street cops work with ninety-five percent of good law-abiding citizens and about five percent of the criminal element. Working undercover as a vice cop, however, one works with five percent of the law-abiding citizens and ninety-five percent of the criminal element.

Debbie and I found that working massage parlors in the division for about three months made us useless. The word was out. We were immediately identified as vice cops when we walked in the place. They knew exactly who we were.

ABC, alcohol and beverage control, violations always took up a lot of our time. It was necessary but violators seemed to get only a slap on the wrist. That's the system. Without some enforcement action, the bars and booze distributors would run rampant.

We received constant complaints regarding the bar at Gaffey Street and Avalon. The home owners on the side streets hated having the bar in their neighborhood so they complained about everything. They alleged the bar served liquor, after hours, to minors and drunks. Simply stated, they just wanted the bar to be closed up.

On the other hand, the bar owner detested the neighbors who complained. They wanted the neighbors on the side street to move.

Debbie and I had to operate on facts, not on who wanted what. In LAPD the Form 1.18, the Vice Investigation Request Report, was the formal way a vice complaint was recorded into police records. That case can not be closed out until the investigation is completed.

On the first night of our investigation, we arrived at the bar at 12:45 a.m. and sipped on a beer, which I really didn't like. The bar closed at 1:55 a.m. sharp. There was no after-hours serving. We checked it on three different occasions during the next seven days. Nothing.

No drunks or minors were served. We even observed the bartender checking a couple ID's of young people. It turned out they were of legal drinking age. We knew they were because we had a black and white with uniform officers stop them after they left the bar. The officers found probable cause to make the stop, but they didn't cite them for anything. This just helped us verify their age.

On our fourth visit to the bar, we discovered that the bartender was probably watering his drinks. We observed that when he finished a vodka or gin bottle he did not break them as is required by ABC law.

The bartender would take bottles he did not break, as required by law, and fill them with water. He either skimmed the money and put it in his pocket or he stole the real booze that his cash register showed was a sale. Either way, he violated the law and committed a theft from the customers who didn't get what they paid for.

When Debbie and I identified ourselves as police officers the bartender denied that he failed to break a bottle. He was a little surprised when Debbie walked behind the bar and pulled three different bottles that contained only water or at least half water. We took the bottles, sealed them with evidence tape over the top and sent them to Scientific Investigations Division's crime lab for analysis.

Five months later, the bartender appeared in court and pleaded guilty. He paid his small fine and went to work for another bar.

After two more continuances, which added another four months on the time table, the California Alcohol and Beverage Control Board suspended the bar's liquor license for thirty days because this was the second incident over a two-year period. By the time the ABC Board heard the matter, the bar owner had probably forgotten what he was cited for.

One night the lieutenant gave Debbie and me the assignment to investigate a 1.18 about gambling at the residence located on 77th Street near the oil fields. The specific complaint stated six males played cards three times a week at the same location.

We went to the location and sat in our unmarked police car across the street from the house. The front window curtains were open and we could see six men sitting at the dining room table. They were playing something. We got out of the car and walked to the sidewalk and then we had a clear view of the card game. It was just before midnight and the front door and windows were open. We could hear the bets called, checked and who the winner was and what cards he had. The six men included three blacks, two Caucasians and one Latino.

I told Debbie I would take the front door if she would enter the back. Our plan was to wait sixty seconds and both enter at the same time. We called for backup.

At the precise moment I entered the front door with the usual quick knock, yelled "Police, open the door," waited about ten seconds and then entered.

The six men remained seated, but they all looked extremely large, far taller and heavier than Debbie or I. They looked like a group of dock workers who were really upset with their poker game being disturbed. They were not impressed with my badge and my gun was in the holster, under my shirt that hung outside my jeans.

I said, "You are all under arrest for gambling. Put your hands on the table and remain seated!"

All of a sudden the largest man at the table jumped up and said, "You will have to whip me if you plan to take me to jail."

By now, I really wished Debbie was here. Then I heard banging on the back door, then it stopped. Another thirty seconds and she ran in the front door just in time to hear the conversation.

The real big guy who happened to be black and looked like he could eat me for breakfast, said, "You may be the vice but do you think you can take me?"

I swallowed a couple times, then realized my mouth was getting real dry. I knew I had to act quickly.

After a heavy silence of ten seconds or so, my reply was, "I'm sure you can whip me real good. You are big and you are tough. But, I promise you this, after you whip me, I'll have eight thousand other officers out here on the streets, looking for you as long as it takes to find you. Then you will be arrested, booked and sent to prison for a long time charged with whipping a police officer. This is a serious violation of the California penal code. It is also a violation of the contempt-of-street-cop statute. Now, do you want to whip me or surrender?"

I figured this guy was going to beat me senseless and then Debbie was going to question me about the crazy violations I had verbalized.

Then one of the other black guys stood up, and said, "You will have to whip me and the other four guys here, if you even think about whipping this officer."

At first I thought he was talking to me, but then I realized the second man was telling his fellow card player to leave me alone. After that, they all submitted peacefully to their arrest and we called for a couple of black and whites to transport them to the station for booking.

All six were booked and released with a small amount of bail. I cornered the man who had stood up and asked him why he defended me.

He replied, "First, my buddy had too much to drink, he really isn't a bad guy. Secondly, about two years ago you arrested me for gambling. I was shooting dice in the alley near 9th Street and Figueroa when you were working as a foot beat cop. You treated me with respect and just did your job. I wanted my friends to treat you with respect. Third, the fine will only be fifty dollars. It ain't no big deal."

After all the dust cleared at the house, we found that the rear door had been barred with a two-by-four board. There was no way an officer could have kicked the door in, even at the point of least resistance, near the door handle. The key to the city would not have let Debbie in their rear door.

After Debbie and I were recognized in most of the massage parlors, bars we worked for ABC violations, and poker and dice games, the lieutenant assigned us a task of working a bookie that owned a bar. The bookmaker-bartender owned and worked in a small bar at 25th Street and Dana Point Drive. We had never worked the bar for ABC violations so the lieutenant figured the bookie would not recognize us as the "heat."

The horse bookie owned the bar, worked as the bartender and took all the horse racing bets in person. These bets were as small as one dollar and went up to five hundred on a single race. They passed the bets off to a "back room" via phone. The backroom operation was not even near the bar. All the bets from a number of hand-kept books were passed back to the central location, which was often operated and financed by organized crime.

We both dressed in our grubby clothes and went to the bar several times over the next two weeks. Each time we took a Racing Form and discussed the bets we were going to make loudly enough so the bartender could hear us.

Neither Debbie nor I were big drinkers so we just sipped our drink or dumped half of it on the floor, in a planter or in the toilet. It was like a game to figure out how we could get rid of the beer without the bookie realizing what we were doing.

On our second trip to the bar, Debbie came up with some kind of Tupperware cup and tight lid that she carried in a big, ugly purse. We could rid our drink in this.

The next time we went into the bar, I tried to outdo Debbie by wearing a pair of old cowboy boots. The boots were a size 13 on my size 10 feet. They gave me just enough room for a half of a bottle of beer to slosh around in. Debbie thought it was funny. I only did that once because it was like taking a bath in a T-shirt.

On the third trip to the bar, I asked Benny Harrison, the bookie-bartender, where the pay telephone was. He directed me to the rear of the bar near the restroom. Then I went to the phone and pretended to be making a bet with a bookie. He passed by me a couple of times and I talked softly to conceal my illegal betting.

Actually I was checking in with Marie and the kids before they went to bed. Marie thought it was funny that I was pretending to be placing a bet. I think she liked to be involved and I know she was not thrilled with my having a female partner. I kept telling Marie it was necessary in this kind of work. It would be too obvious if two men walked in together. Both Debbie and I thought Benny was on to us. We saw betters enter the bar, exchange money like a dope buyer and leave the bar. The bookie made notes on small pieces of paper which were destroyed when placed in water or any other type of liquid.

The bookie never offered to take our bets. He knew we were supposed to be betting as we made it quite obvious.

At the end of three weeks we were just about to give up on this approach when he walked over to our table and said, "Can I sit down?"

I said, "Sure. Can I buy you a beer?"

He sat down but told me no thanks for the beer. He cut to the chase very quickly. He said he knew what we were doing and we played dumb, real dumb.

Debbie and I thought Benny was going to talk about the disposing of our beers or that we were undercover cops, but then he said there was no need for me to place our horse racing bets over his phone. He offered to accept it for us and save us a dime. This was the break we had been waiting for.

For the next two months we placed two or three bets each day the horses were running at Santa Anita Race Track. Another team from

Ad Vice, Administrative Vice Division, who were the organizational heavyweights, worked with Organized Crime Intelligence Division to make a case on the back-room organization.

Things were really going well and we were having a lot fun. Then Debbie's number came up on the sergeant's list. She was promoted to sergeant. She was as happy as could be, but because we were involved in this big bookmaking investigation, our Lieutenant Allen worked it out with the hierarchy to leave Debbie's name off the published transfer list as she was undercover.

Because Debbie was working undercover, she went down to Parker Center via the back gate and met with the chief. He privately congratulated her and gave her the sergeant's badge. He was going to assign her to Wilshire Division working as a patrol supervisor on the morning watch. However he authorized her to be loaned back to Harbor Vice until the secret investigation was concluded.

This was like getting her ticket punched. The chief had given her an unlimited loan on the investigation and her probation clock as a sergeant was running. Even with all this good luck, the most important thing was she was avoiding the morning watch as a young sergeant.

Her new captain would never bring the subject up to get her loan terminated and brought back to his division because the chief had blessed it once. Her new boss was quite ambitious and would never question the chief's direction, even if the loan went on indefinitely.

The captain at Harbor Division would milk her loan out as long as he could. He had Debbie as an extra sergeant working vice. This captain wasn't looking to get promoted, he was a workaholic and liked to have his cops make lots of good vice arrests. Debbie had the best of both worlds.

The hot shots from Ad Vice worked on the case for another six months. Debbie and I kept making book with Benny until they could get an airtight case. We were no good at picking horses and kept losing most of the time. Benny loved it.

Then one day Lieutenant Allen called Debbie and me out of the field to his office. To our surprise he had ten cops from Administrative Vice Division, including their lieutenant. Today was to be the "A-Day" for this caper. The "A" was for arrest.

The plan included our team's placing a bet with Benny five minutes before the fifth race. Both of us wore body wires and our conversations were being monitored and recorded by the team. Thirty seconds after Benny phoned the bet to the back-room operation, we were to make the statement "The bet is in."

This message was then relayed to the other eight cops who were waiting around the corner from the back-room operation. The operation went down like clock work.

Six bookies were arrested at the scene, but the best part was the quickness of the team because they were able to recover all types of evidence. A couple of cops from Organized Crime Intelligence Division showed up at the back room and were eventually able to prove the bookie's connections with organized crime.

Lieutenant Allen allowed us to take Benny into custody but let us avoid booking him. He couldn't believe we were cops. He had gotten to know us so well, he was just about to invite us to come to his house for a home-cooked meal. Actually, Debbie and I had grown to like Benny.

We cut a deal with him and no one ever realized he was the cause of the raid on the back room. If they had ever figured it out, Benny would have been dead meat. The information he turned was well worth his free ride.

Benny was good for Harbor Vice for a long time, but he finally went broke because he could no longer operate as a bookie. Later, I learned that Benny sold the bar and moved up near Fresno.

When the matter went to court, we got convictions on all of the back-room defendants except one. He went free because he turned Ad Vice onto some better book making operation. Debbie was able to continue undercover for another six months, which got her off her probation. She finally went back to Wilshire Division and was assigned to the morning watch. After just one month in uniform on the morning watch, Debbie was recruited to work Ad Vice. I couldn't believe it; they needed a female sergeant with some expertise in bookmaking. There weren't many females in LAPD at that time who had developed that specialty. Debbie, once again, beat the system.

10

KIDDY COPS

After a little more than ten years in uniform and a tour of Vice, I landed a job at Juvenile Division. The street slang for the assignment was "Kiddy Cops." We worked on the first floor of Parker Center. I knew the building and the people as well as the back of my hand. The cafeteria still belonged to the brass after 9:00 a.m. However, the more ambitious officers at Juvenile Division liked to be visible to the brass, so they occasionally wandered up to the eighth floor for a cup of coffee and a sweet roll.

Parking at Parker Center was now much better, however, Central Division had relocated to their new building at 6th Street and Wall Street.

When one first arrived at Juvenile Division, the Captain called you into his office and made a big deal of his indoctrination program. He required every new officer to be rotated into each of the five sections in the division for a one-month period.

His program gave everyone a chance to be exposed to all the jobs in the division. At the end of the five months, the captain would then assign the officer to a section where there was an opening. This was where he wanted the officer assigned, not necessarily where the officer wanted to go. It was called management's prerogative.

Juvenile Division was responsible for city-wide jurisdiction over selected juvenile-related crimes. It seemed that everyone ended up being permanently assigned to the Child Abuse Section, which was the backbone of the division.

The Administrative Section handled various administrative matters for the division. One project we did was to rewrite and update the department's Juvenile Procedure Manual. This job helped me on the sergeant's examination. Two questions on the test came directly from the manual.

The Youth Services Unit coordinated all the LAPD youth programs including the Law Enforcement Explorer Program, which runs an academy for the young people. It paralleled the police officers training and is held at the Police Academy.

The Operations Section maintained liaison on all juvenile-related matters with the eighteen geographic coordinators in the city. We worked at maintaining liaison with other city, county, state and federal agencies.

The Child Abuse Section is the most sensitive assignment in the department. It required understanding, compassion and special sensitivity for children. Officers deal with cases of physical and sexual abuse of the worst kind.

There are organized groups that believe there is nothing wrong with a person having sex with a child. As repulsive as it may seem, the only thing they see wrong is the law prohibiting such acts. These groups openly lobby to change the law to make the sex acts with a minor legal.

Juvenile experts identified evidence of a cycle in child abuse. It appeared that parents who were themselves abused as children were substantially more likely to abuse their own children.

The chief proposed the implementation of a new method to be used in combating child abuse. He called the proposal "P and E," Prevention and Education. It included family counseling, social welfare services, follow-up systems and programs, conducting classes for everyone involved, legislation and media programs, as well as twenty-four-hour services available for help. Unfortunately, due to lack of funding, the program was never completely implemented.

It didn't take me long to see that parents and public education had failed when it came to uncontrolled children. I faulted parents first, but felt public educators had to share in the blame. If parents, educators and society didn't start to take a stronger interest in and concern for young people, I knew that in the future serious problems would be evolving and erupting.

I felt that our educational system had failed when young people were becoming disrespectful to adults and using all types of drugs and alcohol. I believed the parents and the schools had not exercised enough discipline or control. Marie said I was too rigid on this matter, but I still would not bend. Maybe she was right. Sometimes it was society and peer pressure that were partially to blame, yet young people need strong discipline and a "tough love" concept.

The closest thing to street-police work at Juvenile Division was working in the Juvenile Narcotics Section. We provided juvenile narcotic enforcement throughout the city. An excellent school-buy program in cooperation with the Los Angeles Unified School District was in place. Each semester twelve undercover officers were placed in different high schools. The officers were monitored closely.

The officers working the undercover school buy program had to look exceptionally young. With my time-in-grade and seniority, I wasn't qualified for the job. However, I was assigned to the unit for two weeks in order to learn how the supervising officer worked each case. These officers see some mind-blowing behavior. Young people cook their brain on drugs and create a terrible learning environment.

The officers often make ten to twenty buys from a single student who is selling drugs on the school campus. What a waste of the human mind. The police and the schools are working to improve the situation, but it often seems we're losing the war on drugs.

The DARE, Drug Abuse Resistance Education, Section was another joint venture with the school district. This program put uniformed officers in the classrooms on the school campus to teach children to say NO to drugs. It was highly effective.

While I worked this section, I was assigned the task to go to at least five different community service clubs and any other organizations that dealt with youth, and give presentations to help raise funds for the program. I gave a motivational speech on how we had to take the profit out of narcotics crimes and the need to train kids to turn away from drugs. They apparently liked my speech as my efforts helped raise more than ten thousand dollars for the program.

One of the saddest cases I experienced while working Juvenile Division involved a couple living in the Hollywood area. Both David and Mary Shafer worked and were successful in their professions. The entire family was, at one time, quite involved in their church activities. As the children grew older and the parents became more involved in their outside social activities, church attendance and commitment began to slacken.

The Shafers had three boys. The oldest son, Peyton, was twenty years old, attending the state university and was a varsity football

115

player. He was a straight "A" student and had never been a problem to the parents. He drove his five-year-old Ford Explorer and was as happy as could be.

The second child, Scott, was eighteen years old. He graduated from West Coast Military Academy where he was also an "A" student. He excelled in sports and was never cause for worry to his parents. He was now a freshman at the U. S. Air Force Academy and planned to be a pilot. As he lived at the military academy during high school and was attending the academy, he had no need for a car.

The third son, Jason, was their big headache. He was sixteen years old and had done well at Point Cove High School until his junior year. He got his driver's license the day he turned sixteen. Then the problems really began to escalate.

For his birthday, mom and dad gave him the keys and pink slip to a brand new black BMW convertible. He loved the car and all of his acquaintances at school immediately became his best buddies. They loved the sharp car, and he took them everywhere. He liked his newfound social life. Later the Shafers found out his friends did not have the same family values they had tried to teach their children.

As David and Mary Shafer grew older, they did not screen their third child's friends as closely as they had the first two children. They also found they were more permissive with him.

The Shafers were more successful than ever in their careers. They made more money than at any time in their lives and had more material wealth than ever before. They were heavily involved in charitable and political causes along with their friends in their new socioeconomic circle. They figured they never had any difficulties with their first two children as they grew up, so why worry.

One Friday night, Jason was going to a high school football game then out for dinner with three of his friends. He assured his parents he would be home by midnight.

By 1:00 a.m., his parents were becoming concerned. By 2:00 a.m. they were really worried. At 3:00 a.m. they were panicked and called Hollywood Division.

At 3:20 a.m., a Hollywood Division patrol unit spotted a new black BMW with the top down, traveling at about sixty-five miles per hour, in and out of traffic, heading westbound on Sunset Lane toward the Pacific Ocean. At Doheny Lane, the light turned red for east and west-bound traffic.

Jason was having a great time partying and failed to stop for the red light. He "T-boned" a couple in a Honda turning left in front of him. The Hendersons were just returning home from Westside Community Hospital where they had admitted their only child, a teenage boy who was a polio patient.

The Hendersons were killed instantly as their new Honda was cut in half and no longer resembled a car. The firefighters needed to use the "jaws of life" to get them out of their car.

The BMW looked like an accordion in the closed position. Jason and the young girl in the front passenger seat were killed on impact. Upon further investigation, no seatbelts were found to be in use.

The young boy and girl in the back seat didn't have seat belts on either and were thrown more than a hundred feet onto the roadway. The girl died on the way to the hospital and the boy would be a vegetable for the rest of his life.

Hollywood Division contacted Juvenile Narcotics because dope was found in the car. They also requested that we make the notifications to the involved families.

Autopsies showed a large amount of cocaine in the three killed in the BMW. Also, it showed that Jason's girlfriend was six months' pregnant. His parents had no idea he was involved in dope and a sexual relationship. They had been too busy with their own activities to notice some definite and obvious changes in Jason's life.

Had they spent more time with him, talking with him, doing things with him, they would have noticed his restlessness, not feeling well, irritable attitude, becoming agitated very easily, cutting classes, grades falling, not to mention lots of miles on the odometer of the new car. Too much time was being spent in the car and away from classes at school.

It was later learned that the boy in the back seat had a record with the LAPD. He had been arrested by one of the undercover officers working the school-buy program two years earlier. This same young man had sold rock cocaine to the officer on thirteen different occasions before we had our airtight case. He was arrested but ended up getting "slapped on the hand" and suspended from high school for about a year and a half. He had returned to school four months before the accident.

The pain and suffering this one incident caused cannot be described. It was devastating. So many people and families were affected.

Later we learned the civil liability, which was secondary to the case, was disastrous. The Shafers' liability exceeded their automobile insurance policy limits. Eventually, they declared bankruptcy. The family was shattered, financially and emotionally.

After this incident, I concluded that there are seven deadly sins that get people, especially kids, into trouble. They are: wealth without work, pleasure without conscience, knowledge without character, commerce without morality, science without humanity, worship without sacrifice and politics without principle.

Another narcotics-related investigation took place in late September. One day our supervisor, Sergeant Erik Schroeder, received a call from the MVS, Major Violator Section, of Narcotics Division. In the LAPD, this section was often referred to as the "Elephant Hunters." They only wanted to work major enforcement cases and always tried to kiss off any dope work that wasn't big.

This section seemed to get all the glory. The garbage cases were passed down to less prestigious units that worked dope. This practice really was a sensitive issue with the Kiddy Cops, who also viewed their own work as important.

Sergeant Schroeder said there was a report that juveniles were working as "swampers," unloading trucks, in the Los Angeles Produce Market and selling dope in the area. Schroeder grabbed Rob Martinez and me and we headed down to Olympic and Alameda.

We met with one of the produce business owners at the corner coffee shop. We sat in one of the back booths and tried to stay out of the public view as requested by the man. He identified a young male named William Michaels as our suspect. The juvenile suspect was supposed to be selling marijuana and cocaine to a number of the workers in the market area.

Our information included the allegation that the suspect worked as a swamper, but sold dope in the area between 10:00 p.m. and 4:00

a.m., Sunday through Thursday, when the produce trucks were being loaded and unloaded.

We thanked him for his help and then, as usual, reassured him that we would never disclose his identity as our informant.

Erik Schroeder was a young, energetic and ambitious sergeant who couldn't wait to be transferred to the MVS. Then, he hoped to get promoted to lieutenant. He would never admit that this was his motivation but everyone working for him could read it on his face and in his actions.

Before we left the coffee shop, but after the informant had left, Erik looked us in the eye and said, "You can have all the overtime you need, but I want these drug sales in the produce market cut off completely. I want a 100% no-tolerance policy on dope sales here. When you make an arrest, immediately notify me, as I want to be involved in the interview. Do you have any questions?"

Rob replied, "No, sergeant. We understand you completely."

At the same time, Rob kicked me under the table which meant "Here we go again!"

For the next three nights, we dressed in grubby old work clothes and mingled around the large produce market. We played the part of a worker in the area. Because the market was so large and there were so many workers, we fit in well. No one suspected we were cops.

After tracking the suspect for three days we knew his modus operandi (M.O.) quite well. We watched him talking with many drivers and laborers. His M.O. was to exchange small plastic bags that he pulled out from his old U. S. Army field jacket. The large pockets permitted him to hold a lot of dope, which showed a lack of experience on his part. A wise trader never carried more than enough for one transaction.

He appeared to sell dope to anyone who came to the truck where he was unloading the produce.

With that, Rob said, "Let's give it a shot!"

On the third morning, at 3:55 a.m., Rob walked up to the young fellow, made some small talk, then said, "Give me a bag of coke," and handed him a fifty-dollar bill.

The suspect pulled out a wad of bills that was more money than Rob and I together earned in a month. The suspect handed back the change and a bag of coke and then Rob turned and walked away.

When all this happened, I was situated in a spot where I could hear and see the deal go down. We had a body wire on Rob so we got it all on tape.

About 4:30 a.m., as the suspect left the produce market in his car, we followed him for about twenty blocks. Then we had a black-and-white unit stop him.

The uniform officers approached him about his rear stop light lens that was cracked. We walked up and relieved them. We cuffed the suspect, read him his rights, parked his car on a side street and transported him to Parker Center.

As Schroeder had directed, we called him so he could get involved. We figured he wanted to share in the glory of the investigation, get his name on the arrest reports or maybe he needed the overtime money.

To our surprise, Erik was in the interview room with us within forty minutes. The suspect wasn't a juvenile. He was an eighteen-year-old, male Caucasian, five-feet-eight inches, one hundred sixty pounds and a high school dropout. He was trying to make quick money.

Working as a swamper six hours a day netted him about forty dollars on his W-2 or about ten thousand dollars a year, well below the poverty level.

On the other hand, working as a dope dealer netted him about four hundred dollars a day or about one hundred thousand dollars a year. He didn't earn social security credit on the latter nor did he pay taxes on the earnings. All of this profit was contingent upon someone such as Rob and I not screwing up his good deal.

With only three weeks' experience selling dope, William didn't exactly set the world on fire. His survival rate on the streets was not good. It was a risky business, to say the least, and his M.O. showed little or no caution.

Rob took the lead in the interrogation of Michaels. They went round and round with peripheral talk about the dope operation and his involvement. We were surprised as he was actually quite naive and copped out to everything. This was highly unusual.

William's boss had hired him with the understanding that he was a minor, meaning he was under eighteen years. When he was hired he was seventeen years old, but a week later he had a birthday and turned eighteen.

The smart dope dealers liked to use kids that were minors as they would only get a slap on the hand if the juvenile got caught.

William was far more naive than his boss could imagine and this kid liked to talk. Schroeder was foaming at the mouth. He couldn't wait to put in his two cents' worth.

Finally, the sergeant took over and wanted to cut to the chase. Within twenty minutes he had promised he would kick William loose, return his complete wad of money, less Rob's dope-buy money and pay him five-hundred dollars from the Juvenile Narcotics Buy Fund, if William informed us about a big deal about to happen which would be a large dope bust for us.

The Narcotic Buy fund money came from an asset forfeiture account and was like free money, at least for the sergeant, but we had to account for it like a kid going to the store to buy milk with a five-dollar bill. Obviously, the sergeant had a lot more discretion than we ever imagined.

Rob and I looked at one another. We couldn't believe the sergeant would authorize such a deviation from what we believed was clear-cut department procedure.

However, the sergeant did it and told William he would give him a free ride until we made our big bust, then he was to leave town or risk the consequences of being identified as our narcotics informant. This was like a death sentence and the kid now understood it. His dope career in L.A. was being cut real short.

Schroeder promised if the information were not correct, he would find him, book him and guaranteed him at least ten years in San Quentin. William believed him and we couldn't get him to stop talking. During the next four hours, he told us information that would have taken us about nine months to develop.

Then the sergeant instructed us to drive Michaels back to his car and send him off in good spirits. We complied.

En route back to Parker Center, Rob said it was obvious. This big bust was to be Schroeder's ticket to MVS. Why else would an ambitious guy such as the sergeant take such a risk? Internal Affairs would burn him in a minute. We figured we would be his "boys" from now on. He would never want us to cross him.

When we got back to Parker Center, the sergeant was waiting for us. He said we should forget the contents of his interrogation of William Michaels. We acknowledged that we understood. Then he gave us his plan.

Tomorrow, Thursday, Rob and I were to leave Parker Center at 3:00 p.m. and travel over the Grapevine toward Bakersfield via Highway 99 and take the Pumpkin Willow off-ramp, then go eastbound approximately four and a half miles to the Texaco service station. We were to wait around the gas station and coffee shop until 6:45 p.m.

At 7:00 p.m., a new Peterbilt truck, either orange or yellow in color, with a double-wide sleeper and chicken lights and pulling a forty-four-foot Great Dane reefer would pass by the station heading eastbound and travel less than a mile to a produce packer on the north side of the highway. The truck would be loaded with twenty-three pallets of boxes of lettuce in the rear of the trailer using a forklift.

Schroeder continued with the description of what we had already heard from William.

"Just before the trailer is to leave, a small reefer van will arrive and the twenty-fourth pallet will be lifted off with the forklift and placed on the right rear of the trailer. This pallet will contain lettuce, but in the center of the pallet there will be six boxes of fine-cut cocaine. The six boxes will look like lettuce boxes except they will contain Styrofoam with the coke inside these waterproof boxes."

The prize would be five hundred eighty pounds of coke with a street value of twelve million dollars. William had picked this up when he was hiding between two of the trucks before his boss, the big dope dealer, hired him. He said it was like clock work every Thursday night and the truck would pull into the produce market at exactly 10:00 p.m. to be unloaded. The first pallet unloaded was the one that was the target.

Well, the bust would not be the biggest, but certainly would be large enough to qualify the sergeant for an MVS case. If we were successful, it would be worthy of at least a commendation.

The sergeant wanted us to watch the entire loading, count the pallets, follow the truck back to the produce market and watch where the dope pallet went. He would be waiting at the market with a team of ten Juvenile Narcotics officers. When the dope was about to be lost in the shuffling of pallets, we were to notify him by radio and he would lead the swoop in to scoop up everyone connected in any way.

Rob and I would ensure the continuity of the evidence from the produce shed in Pumpkin Willow to the point of the arrest and confiscation of the evidence.

We assumed the sergeant would have John Jefferson, his contact in the news room, on alert and the media would be there in a flash. When MVS flipped out at Schroeder for not turning the case over to them, he would quietly remind their captain that the entire matter had been passed off to Juvenile Narcotics by them.

The captain would greatly appreciate Erik Schroeder for not embarrassing his division with the "kiss-off" factor. In other words, Eric would keep his mouth shut, thereby becoming a team player and soon be on the transfer list to MVS with all the overtime he could possibly ever want!

Rob and I came in early, gassed the vehicle and ensured that our spare tire was in good condition. We reached the south side of the Grapevine by 3:00 p.m. We didn't want to get into Los Angeles's notorious 5:00 p.m. traffic.

At 4:30 p.m. we were eating dinner at the truck stop at the top of the Grapevine in Gorman. We kept one eye on the highway to see if we would see a new orange or yellow Peterbilt tractor with a Great Dane reefer traveling a little early to Pumpkin Willow. We never saw one.

By 5:30 p.m. we were about one hundred yards from the Texaco gas station which was just down the road from the produce shed. We pulled over to the right shoulder of the road, I jumped out and ran to the left rear tire of our vehicle and stabbed it between the tire treads with an ice pick, just as I had learned from the South American Organized Crime suspects when I walked the foot beat.

This produced a slow leak. We sat in the car for about five minutes then got out and opened the trunk lid and fiddled with our jack. We acted like a couple of people in real trouble for another five to ten minutes.

Then we put the jack back in the trunk, slammed the lid and drove on the flat tire into the service station. It was a small rural station with only two gas pumps, one repair bay area and a "good ole boy" in overalls. The attendant looked at us as though this was going to be his big sale for the day.

Naturally, the attendant recommended he put a new tire on the wheel for one hundred forty-six dollars, including installation!

Rob said that sounded like a bargain and left the tire for repair. He asked the attendant to put the spare on for now and said we would return before he closed, or on Friday morning, to pick up the new tire. Rob would pay for it with his Texaco credit card when we picked it up.

I couldn't believe Rob got uptight about the guy's charging him the hundred and fifty dollars for the tire. He had worked in a gas station when he was a kid and had taken advantage of "out-of-town folks" in the same way.

Later, I got Rob laughing about how the fellow was just making a living. Anyway, we never went back to pick up the tire.

We killed about a half-hour until the spare tire was installed. Then, all of a sudden, nearly an hour early, a big, bright orange Peterbilt with a double-wide sleeper, chicken lights and pulling a white forty-four-or forty-five-foot Great Dane reefer went whizzing by eastbound with his twin stacks smoking.

Rob Martinez was a funny cop. He loved to work dopers and was a good partner. He made me laugh. As the Peterbilt passed, he said, "Now that boy has a five and four."

I surmised he meant the stick shift in the truck but I didn't admit to my ignorance.

Rob continued with, "He definitely has a four-fifty-seven rear end, and he loves to play with his jake brake. Look at him smoke!"

I nearly split a gut laughing. How in the world would Rob come up with such a line. He was convincing and perfect for working this undercover case. The station attendant also seemed to be impressed.

I didn't even know what chicken lights were, but after the explanation of the truck's gears, rear end and rake bake or whatever, he could get me to agree with him on just about anything regarding an eighteen-wheeler.

Rob told the attendant we would see him later as we got in the car and headed eastbound. The truck turned left into a small produce shed. We continued past the shed for about a quarter of a mile and turned off our lights, whipped an LAPD U-turn and stopped far to the right of the road shoulder.

We grabbed our night imaging binoculars from our workout bag and, in a crouched position, ran about a hundred yards across the onion field to a large, lone oak tree.

It was dark so we had good concealment from our position. We actually were misfits in the onion field, which always made L.A. cops edgy. We had a special hate for this, but it was where we had to be.

With our binoculars we saw pallets being loaded but we did not count them as Schroeder had told us to do. Rob said we would wing it, as only twenty-four pallets would fit in the trailer. I didn't know how he figured it out, but I didn't ask as he was the eighteen-wheeler and pallet expert on our team.

It wasn't until we were watching from behind the tree that Rob told me he had also worked as a swamper in the produce market after leaving his employment at the gas station before becoming a cop. He had definitely gotten his education at the School of Hard Knocks.

Rob was forty-seven years old and really liked police work. He came on the job late and had eighteen years with the LAPD and four years in Juvenile Narcotics. The LAPD was practically his family. He loved it.

He had five children by his first marriage, two by his second and two by his third. He was in the process of divorcing wife number three as he apparently had fallen in love with a curvaceous nineteen-year-old gal who was a waitress at the Jolly Tamale Café in Hollenbeck Division.

On Rob's first visit to the restaurant, she apparently saw his gun and badge under his jacket and then popped for a free taco, plate of refried beans and a couple bottles of Corona beer. He thought it was love at first sight. Rob had been dating the girl for the last six months.

What I couldn't figure out was how they would ever be able to listen to the same music. If he married this gal as wife number four, and if they had children, as Rob usually did, he would be starting on child number ten. Rob would be drawing his social security checks before kid number ten started high school.

I really liked Rob, but my heart went out for his children. My Marie wasn't impressed at all with the story. She said the kids needed their father's love and guidance on a daily basis. She thought Rob's priorities were badly misaligned.

Soon the small bobtail truck arrived. It was an old red International with about a twenty-four-foot reefer box. The workers used the forklift and removed only one pallet from the truck and placed it on the right rear of the Great Dane trailer, just as William had indicated. The driver of the bobtail truck then left the location.

The Peterbilt driver closed and locked the rear trailer doors. He appeared to set the temperature for his reefer before he started it.

Rob said, "He set it on thirty-eight degrees." Then he started to laugh real hard.

He continued with, "Knowing Schroeder, he will want to know the temperature setting. He'll be checking to see if we are paying enough attention to detail."

The Peterbilt driver pulled out and headed toward Highway 99. As he blew some smoke, Rob said he did it by flipping the small toggle switch on the dashboard that activated his jake brake. My partner said it was a macho thing for truck drivers to do.

I said yeah, but didn't have a clue as to what he was talking about, but I was learning.

We kept the Peterbilt in sight from a distance of about a city block, as we headed toward Los Angeles. We were to maintain the continuity of evidence. As long as the trailer was locked and moving, it could not be broken.

We had forgotten about the CHP weigh station. The Peterbilt driver pulled in and we pulled to the side of the highway. Once again, we used our binoculars to watch his actions.

While waiting the fifteen minutes it took for the Peterbilt to crawl slowly across the truck scales, we called Schroeder on our cell phone. I reaffirmed our ETA, estimated time of arrival, of 10:00 p.m. at the produce market. Schroeder liked to be kept informed.

Soon we were moving again. We continued past Gorman just north of Frazier Park where the driver pulled into a brake check area. We stopped about a hundred-yards back and waited. We could see the driver through our binoculars as he exited the cab with a pipe in his hand, then bumped the sixteen rear tires on the eighteen-wheeler. Rob explained that the drivers do this to detect a flat tire before starting down the steep grade. I just nodded.

We could see the reflection in the driver's side view mirror as he had the interior lights on and was fumbling around with something. We got a little anxious and thought something might be going down. We crept slowly toward the truck with our lights out. By now we could see the driver was pouring coffee from a thermos. No big deal.

Rob said, "Call Schroeder!"

I just laughed.

Soon we were at the bottom of the Grapevine, heading for downtown L.A. From this point to downtown, I made notes in my field officer's notebook that could be used to complete all the necessary crime, evidence and arrest reports.

The truck arrived at the produce market and drove about halfway down the row of businesses and backed into a dock. Unlike the small produce shed, Camelot Produce Company had a trailer-high dock for quick and efficient loading and unloading.

The driver got out, turned off the reefer, unlocked and opened both rear doors and hooked them back to the trailer sides. Just as the driver got the doors hooked, a forklift came roaring down the dock from another produce company. The forklift driver pulled up and scooped up one of the rear pallets then quickly turned left. Neither Rob nor I saw where the forklift came from.

From our location, we could not tell if it was the right or left pallet, but we had to make a decision quick or it would be too late.

We both figured it had to be the one with the dope on it but if we were wrong, we would blow the entire caper. At least we knew it was the first pallet removed.

Rob keyed our radio and announced on our tactical frequency, "23JW12," which was our Juvenile Narcotics unit radio call sign, "Go for the Gold!"

This was the green light for Schroeder to move in. It was a perfect signal considering the produce market was located on "Olympic" Boulevard.

After about a thirty-second delay, Schroeder and his crew moved in just as the forklift turned into the produce cooler at Morena's Lettuce Company.

We netted eight arrests, but the best part was that Camelot, Morena's and JXB Trucking, which was out of Bakersfield, were involved in the conspiracy to buy, sell, transport and possess cocaine.

This resulted in seven of the eight defendants being sentenced to ten to fifteen years in either San Quentin or Pelican Bay. Both were the state's maximum security prisons.

The eighth suspect cut a deal, turned state's evidence and gave us valuable information on another big drug deal. Because he helped us, we let number eight go free. He promised to help us in the future when he learned of anything. He became our number-one informant until he got blown up in a random shooting; or, was it a hit?

As a result of the caper, the LAPD's cut of the asset forfeiture fund was about 2.3 million dollars. This was after the seizure of two produce businesses, a new Peterbilt and a new Great Dane trailer plus nearly three hundred thousand dollars in cash from two different safes.

The asset forfeiture laws knock the wind out of dope dealers. The law was enacted to take the profit out of crime and it worked, usually better than the prison system. The criminals hate asset forfeiture, but the cops love it!

Rob and I received a commendation for our personnel file. There was very little publicity about the incident. Sergeant Schroeder surprised both Rob and me when he turned down an offer to go to MVS. Later, we learned that several years earlier, Schroeder had lost his only son due to a drug overdose. His son was only sixteen years old when it happened. Schroeder knew and hated the destruction dope dealers caused.

Rob and I were wrong about the sergeant. He was a good cop and motivated by vengeance, not ambition.

11

SILVER TONGUE

I had learned a lot from the books and professors at Cal-State L.A. It had taken me ten years of going to college on a part-time basis to earn a bachelor's and master's degree in public administration. The framed certificates were not proof of knowledge, but rather proof of self-discipline. My twelve years of police experience had given me a tremendous insight into life and death issues. These lessons were not included in the textbooks.

Survival after making the wrong decisions in a police situation always matured officers quickly. The gun battle in Griffith Park took place a decade earlier but it still caused me to have bad dreams that were usually work related.

Walking the foot beat in Central Division and working both Newton and Juvenile divisions had been a lot of fun and great exposure to the real world. These jobs were a lot more fun than working as a pencil pusher. Most people never realize what real police work is all about.

Yet, I knew if I wanted to get promoted, I needed to work a variety of assignments, including a stint in the "Ivory Tower." That meant I needed to work in the police headquarters, with the brass. I needed to find a job in Parker Center, above the third floor and with high visibility.

The department had a system of advertising weekly for job openings. However, word of mouth always proved to be a couple of days ahead of the formal notice.

One job opening caught my eye: Legislative Liaison Officer-Office of the Chief of Police. There were about six hundred sergeant positions in the LAPD, but this position was one of a kind.

After a lengthy interview and a favorable recommendation, I was selected for the assignment. Captain Pete Hoover had recommended me for the job to the chief. The chief really didn't care, he just wanted the job done and held Hoover accountable.

There was no other police assignment like this one in the entire department. While the state legislature was in session, I would fly up to the state capitol and follow up on legislation that affected the LAPD. I would lobby; we called it *liaison*, with members of the legislature regarding pending legislation.

The difference between lobby and liaison was the fact that I didn't have an expense account on which to wine and dine the elected officials and their staffs. There were no state reporting requirements for liaison officers, but there was a lot of paperwork and reporting for the lobbyist. Any wining and dining had to be with my money.

When not in Sacramento, I would back up Captain Hoover by attending the Los Angeles City Council and council committee meetings. At these meetings we stated the position of the chief of police on all issues raised that affected the LAPD.

In between the formal meetings we met with members of the city council and their staff to express the chief's position on the important law enforcement issues.

Often Hoover and I were called "Silver Tongue" because our job was to talk. Our tongues were always wagging. The truth of the matter was that we at the LAPD were still reaping the benefits of the Watts Riot.

Until Proposition 13, which was the California property tax limit initiative, became law in June 1978, we could have just about anything we needed. The politicians were afraid to say no to any police requests. Captain Hoover and I enjoyed taking credit for the successes.

One day I represented the police chief before the City Council on a hotly contested issue. The subject was gun control. There were five television stations taping the meeting and debate. I was a little nervous at first with all the bright lights and fanfare.

As I began giving my presentations, it came out much smoother than I anticipated. When I finished my speech, each of the fifteen council members drilled me with questions which helped strengthen their point of view.

The politicians usually had their minds made up on most issues long before any presentation or debate took place. The California Brown Act required public decisions be made in meetings open to the public. Discussion and debate are usually only a show for the public, and in this case for the uninformed and apathetic public.

The public confused "open to the public" with "public meetings." Open to the public meant it was the politician's meeting and the public's right was only to attend. The public had no right to speak on the issue, unless the politicians voted to permit it. The point is, the politicians controlled it.

During "public meetings" the public had a right to be heard, but the presentations were statements, not debate with the politicians. This was the place for public input but no one usually paid attention when the public was speaking. Either way, the general public did not understand the system. Hoover said the elected officials wanted it that way.

On my way back to Parker Center, I thought how gullible the public was about politics and all the speeches the politicians made to them. It seemed that politicians had a poor definition of truth. Truth didn't seem to matter ultimately to them. The politicians operated under a belief that "what people believed was the truth" and what was important.

All the politicians had to do was lie and deny, cheat or steal, stall and delay, but make the people believe it was okay. The spin usually worked, but it bugged me when the truth was not exposed.

Captain Hoover and I were having a cup of coffee one day when he told me, "Brad, it's simple. You want to make the truth crystal clear, but they don't want to make it clear!"

Hoover knew me and the system pretty well.

Two weeks later I received a personal letter at work from Mrs. Dorothy Nichols. She had been my eighth-grade teacher at Palm Junior High School. She was now in her eighties and not in good health.

Her letter had a real humbling effect on me. She complimented my presentation to the City Council. It had been aired on television regarding the gun control issue. She went on to say how proud she was of my success and enclosed a photograph of me when I was in her class. Mrs. Nichols was a very dedicated teacher who always put her students' needs ahead of herself.

Today, there are many dedicated teachers. However, there is a lot of stress put on them by parents, laws and expectations. It seems as though many good teachers are held back by this pressure.

After another cup of coffee, I called my former teacher. She was most appreciative of my call and reminisced about several incidents that had occurred while I was at the school. I didn't remember the names involved, or the incidents for that matter, but I didn't let her know that. I just hoped that my memory would be as sharp as hers if I ever reached her age.

Six months later, I discovered that in order to reduce the number of thefts of business machines such as typewriters, calculators and computers in Los Angeles, the Police Commission had enacted Rule Number 413 governing second-hand office equipment dealers. The rule required business machine dealers in the city to report to the chief of police whenever they sold, traded or repaired a business machine not originally sold by them.

Our burglary investigators said the rule had proved quite effective. The recovery rate of stolen machines had increased dramatically. People who bought them became the victim because we were able to recover them much easier.

After administrative review, the chief of police directed that I lobby for legislation to require reporting statewide. He believed if we took the profit out of stealing business machines, it would be a positive step toward eliminating burglaries of the machines.

As I boarded the plane to Sacramento to push for such legislation, I thought how useless my badge, gun and handcuffs were in this assignment. My tongue and brain would be my only tools for this job.

In California there are 120 state legislators. There are forty state senators and eighty members of the State Assembly, but which one should I select to sponsor the legislation?

Because the only legislator I knew prior to this assignment was Senator William J. Smith from Los Angeles, I decided to approach him. Upon my arrival at the State Capitol, I took a copy of the Police Commission rule and headed for his office. With a little casual conversation and a quick glance at the proposal, he agreed to sponsor the Business Machine Bill. The Senate bill would now have to be worked through both the State Senate and Assembly.

During the next three months, it was a difficult task to get the bill through the Senate Criminal Justice Committee. When the committee chairperson suggested a minor amendment, I was about to respond in the negative and protest loudly.

Senator Smith, who was sitting at the witness table next to me, bumped my knee under the table, leaned over and whispered, "Son, in this committee, be glad to get a half loaf of bread!"

With that information, I answered the chairman, "That would be fine, sir! Yes, sir!" The bill was not perfect but it would accomplish our goal if we could get enough votes in the Senate and Assembly.

The Senate passed the bill on a forty-six to one vote and it was sent to the Assembly. A few weeks later it was heard by the Business and Professions Committee. We finally got it out of the committee and the Assembly voted sixty-eight to six on the matter. It had taken one hundred thirty-seven days from the date the bill was introduced until the date it was sent to the governor. The governor signed the bill and it became law.

On another occasion, I caught an early-morning flight from Long Beach to Sacramento. I wasn't really awake yet, but the trip was a must. A good cup of Couger's coffee even sounded good. I hurriedly identified myself and signed the documents which permitted me to carry my gun on the aircraft.

The purpose of the trip was to testify on several other critical pieces of law enforcement legislation. It was important for me to meet with two or three of our legislators to lobby them on the proposed legislation.

Special interest groups, without the public's best interest in mind, lobbied the other side of the issues. Often it seemed like an uphill battle to fight over things that seemed only reasonable, at least for our position. I guess the lobbyists for special interest groups felt the same way.

I boarded the plane and took the aisle seat in the first row. As I was one of the last passengers on the plane, there weren't many seats left. The PSA flight departed Runway 30, which was a 10,000-foot-by-200-foot slab of concrete, far more runway than needed for the Cessna I usually flew.

As we departed KLGB, which in pilots' speech meant USA-Long Beach Airport, we flew in a northwesterly direction over Santa Catalina Island. As we reached about 5,000 feet in altitude I glanced out the left window and got a good view of the island and saw the Avalon Airport. It brought back a clear memory of the time Keith and I had flown his plane to the island.

Runway 22 was only 3,400 feet long and 100 feet wide but it was like landing on an aircraft carrier. It has a 1,600-foot cliff at the approach end of the runway. I could not see the opposite end of the runway because of the way it slopes upward in the middle of the field. When landing on the island we always get the updraft from the ocean and cliffs. The runway is very rough and has potholes.

When we landed on the island, I was at the controls as the pilot in command, and I landed so hard on the nose wheel, I blew out the tire. We were taught never to do this! I tried to correct it by holding the nose wheel off the ground as we were taught in a soft field landing. I figured Keith was going to end my days of flying his airplane, but he just shrugged his shoulders, smiled and said, "Brad, the second greatest thing a man does in life is "FLY."

I asked, "Well what's the first?"

Keith said, "LANDING!"

We both laughed and Keith told me to taxi over to Island Aircraft Maintenance and get a new tire. He would not let me pay for it. He insisted on paying. He was a generous guy, but I learned a real good lesson that day: Never let the nose wheel touch down first.

As the PSA jet started to penetrate the clouds in our high climb, Catalina vanished and I leaned my head back, closed my eyes and remembered the time Keith and I had flown down to the Palm Springs Airport.

On our return trip, as we neared our destination, I noticed the manifold pressure was approaching the "red line," so I gently pulled the throttle to reduce power. Nothing happened.

I repeated the action two more times, but still nothing happened. Then I pulled the throttle back to the off position. Nothing happened. The throttle was obviously somehow disconnected, but there was no way to check under the hood while in flight. The engine continued to roar and our airspeed was too fast to attempt a landing at Compton.

Keith was a B-52 pilot in the Korean War and had far more flight hours logged than I. He was cool and never got excited, or, at lease he didn't show it. On this day he folded his arms just as he did when I blew his tire out on Catalina Island.

I asked Keith, "Well, what do you think?"

He replied, "Brad, you are the pilot in command. It's your mission. What are you going to do? Make a decision!"

With that, I again concealed my fear and without hesitation squawked 7700 on our transponder and tuned our radio to 121.5, which was the established emergency procedure.

The FAA's radar alarm would go off and they would clear any nearby air traffic. The airlines didn't like to have late passengers, but all pilots were trained to know what to do.

I then broadcast: "Cessna-SkyLane 1112RG, we have an emergency. Mayday-mayday-mayday. We are over Compton Airport climbing to 3,000 feet. We have a stuck throttle and need to land at LAX on a long runway and have emergency equipment standing by."

I knew the plane could glide that far without power if I had calculated the wind correctly. The key was to control the airspeed with pitch, instead of power. *Pitch* meant controlling the up or down position of the nose of the airplane. I would hold the airspeed at seventy knots, no more, no less, which is the best glide speed for Keith's Cessna-182.

The air traffic controller cleared us for an emergency landing on Runway 25L. This was great because it gave us one of the longest runways at LAX, with no potholes.

I think Keith liked to watch me in action under pressure. He liked to see me wriggle and squirm.

When I got within two miles of LAX, I pulled the fuel mixture lever to the cut-off position, turned off both the ignition and magnetos, and glanced at the emergency check list, which reminded me to shut off the fuel flow valve. Then I suggested to Keith that we unlatch our doors for a quick exit if necessary.

As we approached 1,500 feet, I started to skid the plane down to a much lower altitude so I could still clear the obstacle at the approach end of the field. At about 900 feet, I started putting down the flaps in increments of 10 degrees, then 20 degrees, then finally 30 degrees, which produces all the drag possible. I knew the rule that once the flaps were extended they could not be taken off during the landing!

When our airspeed decreased to about forty-five knots, we were then about six inches off the runway, which meant the plane touched down perfectly and with no power. It worked just as I had practiced many times, but I never did it without the option to call it off and activate full power. Also, I had never done it with so much emergency equipment available on the runway.

After we came to a complete stop, Keith said, "Brad, well done. Not only are you a good director of security for me, but you are a decent pilot. However, you didn't need all the fanfare and fire trucks!"

Within a half-hour they had towed us to the aviation repair shop. I had to do all the FAA paperwork on the emergency landing situation.

Just after the PSA jet was reaching about 24,000 feet, I opened my eyes and glanced to my right. In the window seat was one of the legislators I needed to contact.

It was lucky for me. What a fortunate opportunity! For the hour-long flight, I had a captive audience. The senator listened to me and gave me his views on the matter. It was great. He didn't have a chance to escape at 30,000 feet. Later on, this state senator became the governor.

A month later I again traveled to the State Capitol on another piece of legislation. The committee continued the hearing on the matter for a week. As my return flight was scheduled for the next day, I decided to drive my rental car out to San Quentin Prison. I wanted to see the inside of the prison but normally they don't allow anyone, even a cop, in for a tour. This was a challenge for me.

After all, I had indirectly provided some of the residents for the institution. I could think of at least three guys that Randy and I had arrested and ultimately sent them.

I wonder if they remembered me as well as I remembered them. That's exactly why cops don't give out their home addresses and always carry a concealed weapon.

I arrived around 3:30 p.m. on a Wednesday. I walked up to the guard shack at the outer gate and "buzzed" the guard, meaning I displayed my badge with identification card. I told him who I was and asked for a tour of the prison because I'd sent them so many residents.

The correctional officer at the gate chuckled but told me they don't let anyone in or out, without a written order from the warden, I persisted and told him they would be out of inmates if it were not for the good arrests that street cops like myself were sending them. He laughed and let me know he had sufficient prisoners inside that were doing enough time to last his entire career.

After a few more wisecracks he agreed to get his watch supervisor, who could also tell me "No!" Now we both chuckled. I wouldn't let him get his lieutenant until we joked for about five more minutes. I threw in a couple of short police stories.

I could tell he liked the blood-and-guts story of me getting blown up in Griffith Park. I exaggerated the story a little, but he believed it after I showed him my bullet wounds. Maybe I even changed his mind and he asked his lieutenant in a convincing way. After waiting another five minutes, the lieutenant came out to see me. He was an old-timer and obviously ready to retire.

So far I had invested about twenty minutes and hadn't yet made it past the first gate. As a street cop, it seemed as if it was harder to get into San Quentin than to get out.

The older lieutenant and I chatted for a few minutes and I told him a couple of good police stories. I dropped a couple of names and then "bingo." The lieutenant was dealing with my former nemesis Bobby Rossmore on a daily basis. Bobby had become a coke head before he was sent to Quentin. Anyway, I knew this was my ticket inside when I told the correctional lieutenant how I had finally got him off my foot beat. He loved the story, then he told me the truth.

His shift got off at 4:00 p.m., but if I would wait around until his end of watch, he would talk to the night-watch lieutenant that would be relieving him. Because the warden would be gone by the change of watch, the night-shift lieutenant might deviate from the no-visitor rule. Then, I'd be inside in a flash.

My waiting paid off and shortly after four o'clock the two lieutenants came out and I was introduced to Lieutenant Fernando Sanchez. Yes, the "silver tongue" had prevailed again.

Almost immediately the lieutenant took me to the top of the wall. From here, he pointed out the east block. This is where everyone starts out. Good, bad or indifferent, they all started out at the east block, which looked like a building in the projects but with many more bars.

Fernando then showed me the north block and pointed out this was the second stop for an inmate. This is the same type building but with not quite as many bars on the windows as in the east block.

He advised me that all the prisoners were working their way to the west block, which was the "honorary block." Here the prisoners could go to the commissary on their own. They could buy candy, cigarettes and magazines on their own. They were not usually locked in their cells until bedtime.

The lieutenant emphasized the fact that the prisoners had to earn the right to be a resident of the west block and their privilege could be taken away in a snap of the guard's fingers. Due process was not followed inside San Quentin.

To many of these convicted criminals, being in the west block was more important to them than getting out of prison. I guess it was a peer-pressure thing. Oh well.

We spent at least two hours walking the wall. Few people, including cops, ever get the chance to do this. I traveled all the way around the prison and noticed there is a small guard house about every forty or fifty yards.

Inside the small guard houses, the correctional officers are armed with a high-powered rifle, shotgun and tear gas guns. They had high-tech cameras and expensive night-sighting binoculars such as the ones LAPD had. Nothing moved on the prison property without these guys knowing about it.

Walking the wall provided me a better insight into the entire correctional system and the view the correctional officers get from within the system. Money could not buy the insight I received. All street cops should see how this system works, but I knew it wouldn't happen.

Then down to the ground level we went. Fernando showed me the north block area where three officers were killed just two years earlier. As a result of the riot, eight prisoners were killed and sixteen prisoners were seriously injured.

There was no doubt in my mind. The correctional lieutenant would not have given up one of his officers for a hundred of the inmates.

Fernando got a little emotional, especially when he confided that the second officer killed was his younger brother. Come to find out,

Fernando had recruited him because the job was supposed to be a good steady job.

My final stop was the gas chamber. They had strict instructions to never let anyone into the open door of the chamber. The doorway had a thin rope across it hooked to each side of the heavy metal doorjamb.

I thought this would probably be my only chance, during my life time, to get inside the gas chamber. At least, I hoped it would be my only chance. I just had to see what it looked like from the inside.

My next tactic was to tell some more police stories, including a story about a cop killing that took place in an onion field years before. I threw in the emergency landing at LAX story, which I think he enjoyed. All cops like action.

I told Lieutenant Sanchez, "Don't you want to go out to the hallway and call your command center and make sure everything is okay? Just for about sixty seconds!"

He winked as he nodded and stepped out of the room. Then I did it. I grabbed the thin rope off the hook and stepped inside. I quickly walked over to the seat and set my bottom down, but I didn't lean all the way back in the chair. It was spooky.

A great idea flashed in my mind. They should march each prisoner through the gas chamber for a view from the old worn chair just before they arrived in their cell in the east block. If they did this, many of the street cops would have fewer problems with these guys after the State Parole Board released them to the streets.

It was only a thought. I jumped out of the chair, quickly moved back outside of the open chamber doorway and replaced the ropes as Fernando returned from the hallway.

Fernando said, "You didn't go into the gas chamber, did you?" He then smiled.

I just ignored him and told him the story of the great Los Angeles earthquake and how Randy and I handled the caper on the forty-eighth floor of the skyscraper. He thought we should have thrown the hand grenade out the broken window. I told him Randy wanted to give it to our lieutenant at Central Division. Sanchez nearly split a gut laughing.

When I returned to Parker Center, I wrote Lieutenant Sanchez a thankyou letter and enclosed a couple of LAPD shoulder patches, badge tie tack and key chain.   Cops always like this kind of memorabilia.

I concluded that the correctional officer's job, regardless of rank, was much like the job of the sheriff's jailers who really wanted to be street cops.

A few months later, Fernando Sanchez and his wife visited me at the LAPD. I gave them the "cook's" tour and arranged for a ride-a-long in Central Division, with a sergeant, in a black and white unit.

Setting up the ride-a-long was no big deal, but it was a toss-up between Fernando and his wife as to who enjoyed it the most. They rolled on a couple of hot calls and both were really excited about it. It confirmed to me that these correctional officers also wanted to be street cops.

That evening Marie cooked us one of her great chicken dinners. The ride-a-long venture was the topic of conversation during dinner. They loved it.

Our friendship grew over the years.

12

THE BICENTENNIAL

When I first took the talkin' job in the chief's office, Captain Hoover took me up to the police cafeteria for a cup of coffee and some career guidance. As I was now working the "Ivory Tower," high visibility and career development were a big deal. At least that's what Hoover said was important, if one wanted to get on the "upward mobility" program.

He added, "Brad, you should apply for one of the police department's educational scholarships. It will be good for you and you'll get some visibility."

What he was really saying was that he had graduated from Northwestern University Traffic Institute and spent one year, at city expense, attending the school in Illinois. His successful completion of the course earned him lots of recognition from the brass.

Hoover felt it was like getting his ticket punched for promotion in the department. He said it gave him one more advantage over others competing for the higher positions. He knew the system well.

The more I got to know Hoover, I figured he probably designed the system. At least he knew how to make it work. He had only twelve years on the job and he was already a captain. He had a masters degree in public administration, a jurist doctorate and had passed the California State Bar examination and was waiting for his license to practice law. Additionally, Hoover was number three on the commander's list.

There was no doubt in my mind, Captain Pete Hoover would someday be Chief Peter W. Hoover. Maybe not chief of the LAPD but at least chief of some department. He knew the system well and was worthy and well-qualified.

I appreciated Hoover's help and counsel and felt that I should take his advice. I submitted my application for the Northwestern University Traffic Institute, but I was not selected. I completed an application twice for the FBI-National Academy. Was there any hope of being selected for one of the schools?

My high school football coach had drilled into my head, "Never, never, give up." He preached, "desire and determination," continually. In fact, it won our team three championships. At the Police Academy, the sign in the locker room read, "The more you sweat here, the less you bleed in the street." In other words, don't give up!

About a year after applying, I received a call that I had been selected to attend the 125th Session of the FBI-National Academy in Quantico, Virginia. The school started in April and went through late June. The graduation was to take place just before our country celebrated its 200th birthday, America's Bicentennial. The 125th session would be called "The Bicentennial Class."

Attendance at the FBI-National Academy should have a positive effect on my career, I thought. I left work early to share the news with Marie and the boys. They were pleased, but didn't share the same high level of enthusiasm that I had.

That evening my friend Fred Sanders stopped by for a short visit. A half-hour later as Fred was beginning to leave, Marie asked if I would go to the market and pick up a quart of milk for breakfast. Fred said he would ride along with me.

At the grocery store, in my usual way, I reached into the dairy case and pulled out the first carton of milk. This was without checking the date on the carton or without reaching to the rear of the case for the freshest milk, as Marie had tried to train me to do. She liked fresh milk. It wasn't that important to me. Maybe it was because I had learned to tolerate donuts and coffee for breakfast.

After getting the milk, Fred asked if I wanted to stop and have a beer to celebrate my selection for the FBI Academy. Fred knew I didn't like beer.

Marie had once told him the story about how I poured my beer in my cowboy boot when I worked vice. After he heard the story, Fred would rib me about it every time he got the chance. That evening, we did our celebrating with an ice cream cone from the drug store. This seemed healthier than his beer offer.

As we headed home on Whittier Boulevard, we stopped at the red light at Studebaker Road. Fred and I were still eating our ice cream and talking when we heard a popping sound. The noise sounded as though it was coming from the Chevron station located on the northeast corner of the intersection; but, at first glance, nothing seemed unusual. Fred insisted someone was setting off firecrackers. After all, this was the bicentennial year for our country. My police instinct said it was gunshots, not firecrackers!

Suddenly the station attendant, wearing a white uniform and that of an old-fashioned milkman, came running out of the station office. He began running for the corner and yelling that he was being robbed.

A moment later, a Hispanic male, came running out of the office. He was carrying a shotgun and ran to a waiting car. The robbery suspect jumped in the waiting car and away they went northbound on Studebaker Road.

At this point, I blew the red light making a left turn to head north on Studebaker Road and stopped at the corner. I yelled out the open passenger's window, "What happened? I'm an off-duty Los Angeles police officer," as I quickly buzzed him with my badge.

The attendant was obviously badly shaken as he fumbled for words. Fred was real cool, but the attendant had panicked.

My mind flashed back to the incident that took place about ten years prior, at Wade's Gun Store near 14th Street and Olive Avenue, in Los Angeles. But this caper was in my hometown, on my own time. There would be no overtime on this one. Maybe, just maybe, because I was off-duty, the on-duty officer would have to complete the necessary paperwork.

Funny, I thought, on-duty or off-duty, I would always get involved. Was this what I was trained to do?

Now I yelled at the attendant, "Get in!"

Fred quickly opened the passenger's door of my two-door car, and slid to the center as the attendant got in. A moment later we were headed north after the two robbery suspects.

Although less than $100 was taken, it was a robbery and shots had been fired. I suddenly realized I didn't have my police radio or a cell phone with me.

Then I realized I didn't have my gun on. I told Fred to get my gun out of the glove box. Fred immediately handed the two dripping ice cream cones to the attendant.

Naturally, the glove box was locked. Now I had to drive with one hand and struggle to get the glove box key off the key ring. Finally, I succeeded. Fred opened the glove box and handed me my four-inch Smith and Wesson and my extra set of handcuffs.

I think Fred was enjoying this trip to the market to buy a quart of milk. It was quite a change from his daily routine of working from behind a desk at his business. He liked the action. He always wanted to be a cop but he made so much money in his manufacturing business, he couldn't afford to be one.

The attendant finally communicated that the suspect had robbed him of all his personal money, as well as the gas station's money. Additionally, the suspect fired at least two shots at the attendant, trying to kill him, but luckily he missed.

I guess the suspect really got upset at the attendant because he had just made a cash drop in the floor safe. Therefore, there was less than a hundred dollars in the cash box. As the take was so poor, the suspect wanted the attendant's money, which consisted of twelve dollars and some change. This was not going to be a big payoff and the suspect was not amused.

When the suspect rechecked the attendant's wallet and found a fifty-dollar bill tucked away, he became irate. At this point he began shooting at the attendant for lying and holding out on him.

Under the circumstances, the victim probably forgot the money was tucked away. He had actually hidden the money from his wife, not from the bandit. After this caper was over, I bet the victim never hid money from his wife again!

We were moving fast northbound on Studebaker Road and gaining on the suspects. They were blowing a large amount of smoke from their vehicle and swerved to miss another car at Rosemead Boulevard. They made a quick right and entered Interstate 5 and were now headed for Disneyland.

I thought what a great comedy Walt Disney could have made from this scenario. Walt would probably have called it, "The Milk Run That Turned Into the Ice Cream Cape," or "How to Celebrate the Bicentennial." Either way, the young victim really looked funny holding two dripping ice cream cones. As in all emergencies, it seemed to be happening in slow motion.

We entered the freeway in hot pursuit of the suspect. I suggested to the victim, "How about throwing the ice cream out the window?" He honored my request and did so.

I continued, "I'm going to let both of you out at the first freeway emergency call box. Quickly call the CHP, California Highway Patrol, and tell them I am an off-duty L.A. Police officer pursuing two robbery suspects southbound on Interstate 5. Describe the suspects and the circumstances and tell them the suspect's car is an old red Dodge. Tell the operator that shots were fired and officer needs help!"

With that, I abruptly stopped and Fred and the victim bailed out. I then sped off in hot pursuit as I still had the smoking Dodge in sight and it was now smoking like a steam engine. His old car was slow and my car was fast.

I thought about the long list of orders I had given before dropping the two off at the call box. I should have told them to just call for help. They could have figured the rest out. Now I was beginning to sound like Sergeant Danny Wolfer.

However, I often had the fear that my worst danger would be my involvement in some police action, while off duty, in plain clothes and without my gun. *This is really dangerous. Another on-duty police officer, working plain clothes or uniform, can very easily mistake me for the suspect and blow me away.* I was really paranoid about this.

My drippy ice cream or even a greasy Tommy chiliburger did not sound the least bit good at this point. I closed the gap between the Dodge and myself.

Suddenly, out of nowhere, a CHP unit jumped on the freeway, just as we passed Firestone Boulevard. He had his reds on and raced into position behind, but slightly to the right, of the Dodge. The smoke was still belching from its exhaust pipe.

Then a thought flashed. What if the officer was stopping the suspects for a smoking vehicle, not because of Fred's emergency call from the freeway call-box? If this were the case, he could get shot and killed.

Then out of nowhere, two more units pulled up next to the primary unit. They were obviously going to keep traffic away from the suspects as the most critical part of this pursuit was coming to a close.

The CHP finally pulled the suspects over and talked both of them out of the car. They used their public address system that is built into the emergency light and siren bar on top of their police vehicles. This was done without a shot being fired. They really did a professional job, as I hung back so as not to get in their way or shot at.

Obviously, Fred's call was successful. The CHP nabbed the bad guys. One of their units brought Fred and the victim to the scene. Everything was perfect and no one was hurt.

As Fred and I headed for home, he said, "Shall we get another ice cream cone?" I declined the offer and we were back home in a few minutes.

Marie wanted to know how it could take so long to go to the market and buy a quart of milk!

During the next two weeks, the family planned a great vacation, at the city's expense. This package even included city travel time. At least, we thought at the time, it would be the greatest trip the family has taken.

In late March, I headed east to Virginia. I arrived at the FBI Academy on Saturday, April 3, a day early. Our plans included Marie and the two boys flying back in mid-June to attend my graduation. Then we would have a great family vacation as we returned home.

While traveling to Quantico, I heard a man on the radio talking about successful people. He said, "All successful people have at least three things in common. They are goal oriented; have a deep sense of responsibility; and have a positive self-image."

I gave serious thought to the remarks and decided I would drill this lesson into the boys when I returned home.

My first impression of the Academy was that the facilities looked like a large hotel. It was a top-notch facility. Each of the buildings is interconnected with enclosed walkways, which earned it the title of "Hamster Hilton." Later I learned that the enclosed walkways were necessary because of the varying outdoor climate at the ultramodern academy. It was completely self-contained.

The facility staff provides the new FBI agent training that is similar to police recruit training. It also houses the famous FBI-National Academy where 250 police personnel from the United States and its territories, attend a 12-week course. There are four sessions conducted each year.

The main classroom building encompasses twenty-three specially designed classrooms and eight seminar-size conference rooms. These rooms feature the latest in audiovisual aids and instructional support equipment including closed-circuit television and a highly sophisticated student response system.

Besides the modern classrooms, the FBI-Academy had the best pistol and rifle range I'd ever seen. The physical training facility was exceptional and included a large indoor swimming pool. It was great for recreation, but it was also used for teaching many water-survival techniques.

The Academy prided itself on the fact that more than 1,000 of the current heads of various police agencies were among the 9,000 graduates of the first 100 sessions. Many of the other 8,000 graduates were on the way up!

The instruction was superb but the best part of the training was the networking and professional relationships we developed from all over the United States. Some of the friendships made lasted a lifetime.

The attendees joked that women, women's cooking and the FBI were the three most overrated things in America. Actually one of the long-term directors of the FBI put together the concept of an FBI-National Academy.

The idea was to get local law enforcement involved in a tight-knit organization like a fraternity. The feds, that is the FBI, could go to local law enforcement to get their help in solving the federal crimes they were investigating. Prior to this, the FBI did not have the street-level contacts among local law enforcement or the public, but they did have a lot of money to put together a program that brought the local law enforcement into the fraternity. It worked just as the FBI director had planned.

My roommate was John Martin from the Stansville Police Department. Being from Texas, he had a deep southern drawl. Living with him for three months gave me a good opportunity to get to know him well.

John was a great roommate and a real professional. After graduating and many years later, John became the chief of police of three different departments. The largest department was more than 600 employees. He was a hard worker and became a true friend.

The officers from the North and West had fun ribbing the southern officers about their accent. The fellows from the South were good sports and took the teasing well. We topped this off by formulating our official southern dictionary. The list included words such as "balls right," which meant "by all rights," and "up air" meaning "up there." One of the best examples was "cheat yet" which meant "did you eat yet?"

It was also interesting to see the way a police officer's vocabulary differs across the United States. For example the "police badge" was referred to as "a tin, the shield, and the buzzer."

The police administrators communicated in different words and had various accents, but all the officers were united in their common goal of providing the best possible police service with the resources they had available.

In our class were representatives from all fifty states, the District of Columbia, Puerto Rico, the U.S. Virgin Islands, Canada, Brunei, the Philippines, Taiwan, Egypt and Thailand. Our class pushed the number graduated to over ten thousand since the FBI-National Academy's started in 1935.

While at the Academy, I found time on some of the weekends to fly as a private pilot in a rental plane. I found the rental planes, which were usually a Cessna-182, were not nearly as nice as the new Cessna that my friend Keith Willard had at the Compton Airport. They were not the same and the flying conditions were different on the East Coast. Maybe the reason was that I missed my good friend Keith and all the flying we did together.

When graduation day came, Marie and the boys traveled to Quantico for the ceremony. After graduation, we spent another week at a family reunion on the East Coast. By the time we returned home, we had visited over half of the states. This family trip was an invaluable shared experience.

I was glad I never stopped applying for the department's educational scholarships. I concluded that endurance builds steadfastness.

When I got back to work, I was assigned to Rampart Division. There was no such division when I first came to work on the department. About five years after I came on the job, the chief took part of Central Division and part of Hollywood Division and created a new division. He called it Rampart Division.

Funny, I thought, I did exactly as Captain Hoover had suggested and my reward to this point was being assigned to a patrol division on the morning watch. Also, I was assigned to a division where I supervised officers in unit 2A97. This radio patrol car now covered the same area that my old 1A1 worked when I was a rookie working in the old Central Division.

The street cops assigned to 2A97 were going to have trouble pulling the wool over my eyes in this area as I knew it well. The young street cops now assigned to work 2A97 had no recollection of the geographic areas ever being part of Central Division.

This signaled me that I was definitely getting older. Maybe I was even ready to be promoted again.

13

FIT OR UNFIT?

Today was Friday, February 2. It was a special day for me as it marked the completion of my twenty-eighth year of service with the LAPD. This meant that my retirement was vested and I would max out on the benefits in just a couple of years. I always planned to work there for thirty years. Besides, I still loved police work.

The department had been good to me, and in turn, I had tried to do my best for the department. It had been a rewarding relationship.

A couple years earlier, the chief of police had issued Special Order #7, which required each commanding officer to evaluate the physical condition of his subordinates. Through a division order, I delegated this responsibility to the day watch commander, a lieutenant, who was in tip-top shape.

The special order enumerated the criteria to be used to evaluate physical fitness. At 4 p.m., like clockwork, all the division's day watch officers assembled on the grass area of the track at the Academy. Regardless of assignment within the department, the academy was always common grounds for Los Angeles cops. It's like going home or returning to our *alma mater* and it always brought back good memories, memories of when we were younger. All of our careers with the LAPD began at the Academy.

Although I had delegated the task to one of my lieutenants, I wanted to watch and participate. The lieutenant finished the four-phase test with the entire day watch in less than an hour. After declaring everyone fit, he dismissed the troops a little early.

Everyone got a flat two hours of overtime for taking the required test, which also included travel time; that is, everyone but me. Captains didn't get overtime. I was there in my workout suit to encourage physical fitness and set an example by taking the test with the troops. The troops liked to try to prove they were in better shape than their superiors.

As I expected, most of the officers did not leave immediately. Some went inside to work out by lifting weights, some played basketball in the gym, some jogged, some took a hot steam bath and a few went to the Academy Club for a beer, or just to socialize. Health, physical fitness and good diet had become more important than booze.

Without much debate, I started a three-mile jog to top off the week. As always, I did my best thinking while jogging.

Many thoughts seemed to pass through my mind. It seemed funny that I was now in a position to judge the fitness of my fellow officers. I recalled a department movie titled, "The Twenty-Fifth Man." The movie emphasized how only one out of twenty-five applicants were actually hired by the LAPD because they were fit to be a L. A. police officer. The standards were high.

As I jogged down the hill on Stadium Way, thoughts continued to flash through my mind. The words "fit" and "unfit" made me remember my experience of becoming a Los Angeles Police officer.

It began in February 1963, when Uncle Sam handed me my "DD Form 214" as I departed Fort Sill, Oklahoma. I had just finished serving active duty. My good friend Sam Morrison and I were westbound on Route 66 heading for his home in Flagstaff, Arizona.

Sam told me how he planned to join the Flagstaff Police Department and finish college. He said it was good starting pay, a good reference when he finished college and the job would allow him to get his education. Not a bad plan, I thought at that time.

Several days later, I was back in Los Angeles reunited with my brother, sisters and parents. When I told my mother I was thinking of becoming a Los Angeles Police officer, while I finished college, I think she was quite shocked. My dad didn't seem to be too surprised. Both thought I had done some thorough research to come up with this career plan.

There had never been a police officer in our family, however, my great-grandfather was a justice of the peace in a small town in Texas, a far cry from the LAPD.

The day after I returned home, I drove downtown to City Hall. Room 179 contained the Personnel Department's public information center. I filled out an application and paid the $1 filing fee. The woman who accepted the application stated I could take the written examination any weekday at 1 p.m.

As it was now 10 a.m., I decided to kill a little time and take the test that day, eliminating an extra trip back downtown. After a leisurely lunch, I read the job announcement for policeman with a starting salary of $475 a month. Not bad pay at that time, especially for a guy just out of the Army without a job.

By noon, I was itching to get started. At 12:50 p.m., they opened the testing room door and let us in. There were about twenty other candidates present. They allowed me to take the test although I would not be twenty-one years old until the following month. I was definitely the youngest one that day and my military haircut made me look even younger. The others competing for the job looked mature, more educated and they appeared to be qualified for the job.

At the end of the two-hour period, the proctor called time. I barely completed my answers and from looking around the room, I could see I was about the last one to finish. Everyone looked so confident as the proctor quickly graded our exams.

Then she began to call the names: "Mr. Smith, I'm sorry, you failed the written; you may take the examination again in six months." Mr. Jones, Mr. Taylor, and so on. Only the last two names passed the written examination and my name was the last one she called. By the time she called my name as passing, I was elated.

The following Saturday I took the physical agility test at the Academy. I passed this phase with no problem. The obstacle course seemed to be the toughest for everyone, especially going over a six-foot wall.

Two weeks later, I took my oral interview. I would never forget one question an interviewer asked me. "How do you feel about taking a human life?" I squirmed, wiggled and told them I hoped as a police officer I would never have to take a human life, but if the decision is to allow the suspect to take my life or take an innocent person's life, without a doubt in my mind, I would take the suspect's life.

A short time later, I found myself outside waiting for the results of my oral interview. Soon the receptionist came out and congratulated me on a fine score and directed me to the next phase of the testing process, which was the medical examination.

The old Central Receiving Hospital at Sixth Street and Loma Drive provided the examination services for police applicants. This process was much like the military. First, hurry up and wait. Follow the yellow line, follow the blue line and fill up the little jar with a urine sample. Army all the way.

Medical examination results are not known for a couple of weeks, but they scheduled me for the psychological evaluation, or personality inventory, as they liked to call it.

Several days later I was in Parker Center. Doctor Gruben passed me on the psychological evaluation and assigned me to an officer in Personnel Division. The officer, Don Richards, was now my background investigator. He directed me on exactly what the department expected on the completion of the forms.

I hand carried the forms back to Officer Richards, a few days later. His job was to screen and investigate applicants to ensure that only someone qualified became "the twenty-fifth man."

Upon completion of the in-depth background investigation, I received a letter from the commanding officer, Personnel Division. The captain congratulated me on being tentatively accepted for the job of Los Angeles Police officer. I was to start training at the Academy on August 23. I was excited and pleased at my new chosen career.

Everything was going well until three weeks before I was to start the Academy. I received another letter from the commanding officer of Personnel Division. He gave me his regrets and informed me that my medical x-ray showed a possible defect in my lower back, and as such, I was disqualified, which meant I was UNFIT!

I couldn't believe it. I knew I was in excellent physical condition and was certified by the U. S. Army, Uncle Sam. In high school I participated in contact sports, including football, where our team had won three championships. I felt rejected, beat, disappointed and extremely depressed.

I explored all avenues of appeal. After spending a lot of time obtaining information on the medical appeal, I learned that if one of the two orthopedic surgeons believed the medical appeal should be granted, more than likely the entire Medical Appeals Board would approve the appeal.

The first orthopedic surgeon said he could not help, so I had one chance left. I remember praying to God to help me overcome this huge obstacle. I hoped He would see it my way on this occasion.

Two long months had elapsed since I received the disqualification letter from the Personnel Division. Next, I went to see the second orthopedic surgeon on the Appeals Board.

When I appeared for my medical appointment at Dr. John Hill's office, I was in the proper frame of mind, thinking: If it worked, great. If it didn't work, I was going to move on.

I believed the LAPD was to be my chosen lifetime profession, not just a job or a simple career because of a good starting salary or a way to finish college. This profession offered responsibility, honor and lots of action. These things really appealed to me.

I made a pledge to myself that if I were given the opportunity to become a police officer, I would give 100% effort, 100% of the time. I repeated this pledge to Dr. Hill as he closely scrutinized my back x-ray, which displayed a possible displacement of a lower vertebra. He said it was possible that I received a slight displacement while playing football in high school.

Finally, Dr. Hill turned to me and said, "Young man, you really want to be a Los Angeles Police officer, don't you?" I replied, "Yes, sir, and I'll be a good one."

Dr. Hill wrinkled his lips and replied, "You are a borderline case, but I'm going to give you the benefit of the doubt and declare you fit." My eyes fogged up and my heart leaped, as I tried to conceal my emotions.

The appeal was approved by the entire Medical Board and I received a letter stating that I was officially hired. I was scheduled for the Police Academy class beginning February 3.

For the ten weeks prior to going to the Academy, I worked out. I had committed myself to Dr. Hill and, more importantly, to God. Now I had to live up to that commitment. While at the Academy, I continued to strive to achieve my goals.

On graduation day, three months after starting class at the Academy, Officer Star congratulated me on the desire and determination shown in my performance. He also congratulated me on my nomination as class valedictorian.

When I got my sergeant stripes, six years after graduation, I went to Dr. Hill's office to tell him about my achievement. To my disappointment, Dr. Hill had died. I wanted to tell him that the chance he gave me was worth more than money.

By now I was about through with my three-mile jog. I took one more lap around the track before going to the locker room for a hot shower and steam bath. I was fit.

A couple years later, I found myself doing the exact same scenario by taking my physical fitness test with the troops at the Academy. Then I took my three-mile jog that I did so often. It felt good, especially at fifty-one years of age. Thirty years earlier, I thought fifty-one was old, but not today.

I had spent nearly four years as a captain and had commanded three different divisions, but I still liked uniformed police work.

Most captains went to work in a business suit. Often, I wore my uniform and became more visible. The best job on the department was still working in uniform on the streets. I liked to get away from the paperwork behind my desk and go into the real world.

In the LAPD, the troops liked to see the brass in uniform and on the streets if they had the confidence that we were not out there to burn them or unjustly criticize their work. Officers felt good if we were there backing them up and giving them a pat on the back for work well done. They liked seeing the captain take the physical-fitness test with them and also out jogging. This was part of the determination of being fit or unfit.

My retirement was coming soon, and I knew it. Marie and I had discussed it in detail. Now, it was not so far away. She had been ready, but I caused the delay.

We wanted to move away from the city. With my thirty years with LAPD, I had a good pension. Marie's twenty-one years teaching in the Los Angeles Unified School District would net her a fair retirement. We thought we could live very comfortably on our pensions. My pension would be paid by the Los Angeles Fire and Police Pension System, LAF&PPS. Marie's pension would be paid for by the State Teachers Retirement System, STRS.

Thinking about our pensions made me think about Mark Allen. It seemed as though everyone in the LAPD was envious of Mark. He was my old lieutenant at Central Division when I was a rookie. He had earned, or engineered, his thirteen sources of retirement income. Many in the department considered these to be Mark's thirteen great riches in life.

Allen had been retired for five years and was double-dipping on two police pensions. He received one from the LAPD, and the other one for his service as the chief of police of a small police department near San Francisco. This one was paid for by the Public Employees Retirement System, PERS. He also received deferred compensation for life from both departments.

After retiring from police work, he served five years as a superior court judge just north of San Jose. He earned a tax-free disability pension from the State Judges Retirement System, which was probably known as SJRS.

His wife retired after teaching in public education for twenty-seven years, earning her pension from STRS. Mark and his wife, Susie, received their social security and Medicare by earning forty quarters of pay, through a small business they jointly owned. While owning the business, they formed a Top-Heavy Defined Benefit and Money Purchase Pension Plan. At age sixty, the pension plan bought a great annuity for each of them.

The eleventh, twelfth and thirteenth sources of income were in the form of three IRAs, two for Susie and one for Mark. The rumor around the LAPD was that Mark had invested the three IRAs wisely. At age 59-½, the money earned from the IRAs purchased three more substantial annuities for Mark and Susie. The annuities would continue for one of them, whichever lived longer. What an incentive to want to live to be a hundred and beat the system.

As I said, guys in the LAPD thought these sources of retirement income were the thirteen great riches in life. During this jog today, they sounded pretty good to me.

When I told Marie about Allen's thirteen great riches she was quick to disagree. She insisted that family, health, attitude, harmony, understanding, an open mind, hope, fearlessness, sharing, a labor of love, discipline, and faith were as important as lots of money. She said Mark Allen's thirteen sources of income represented only one of the real thirteen great riches in life. She also said the other twelve were more than money.

With that last thought, I was back at the eighth-of-a-mile track and ready to take a hot shower and steam bath. I had just been declared fit, but after this jog, I made up my mind I was going to retire at the end of the month.

14

DOPEY

Dopey, real dopey! When drugs get into your system, legally or illegally, they have a weird effect on your mind. It is like a long dream.

The surgery team was covered from head to toe. They would be perfect in a "Bank 211," a bank robbery. No fingerprints. No footprints. No identifiable threads of clothing. No DNA. No facial ID with those cloth masks. Yes a great two-eleven outfit. Actually, they had a lot in common with the typical robbery suspect.

The surgeon was holding me up for about two grand. The nurses, shown on my bill as hospital charges, were holding me up for another two grand. The anesthesiologist also wanted my money.

The anesthesiologist was the equivalent of seven units, which meant seven quarters at the rate of seventy dollars each quarter of an hour, or unit. "Unit" sounded more professional and not as expensive. This was an easy way to hold me up for four hundred ninety dollars for his fee unless he could figure out how to get his overtime.

This guy could do five or six of these a day, especially if the operation was expedited in an hour, I mean four units. Remember, he billed a minimum charge of seven units. No scholarships! No partial scholarships! No discounts! Not even the usual police discount!

However, if the operation lasted more than seven units' worth, he could slip in another unit, or simply stated, add another seventy dollars. It was like robbery. Medical robbery! You should always cooperate with the anesthesiologist, because he is the only one who can get overtime! As the anesthetic took effect my mind began to wander, in and out like a long dream.

As we approached the door, I remembered my former training officer telling me, "Never kick a door with your shoulder." The door should always be kicked with your strong foot as close to the doorknob as possible. He said it was the point of greatest impact and

157

least resistance. If that didn't work he advised me to use the "Key to the City." This key wouldn't fit in your pocket.

The "Key to the City" was a large piece of pipe, about four feet long and ten inches in diameter, with a circular piece of steel plate on the end. The long pipe had handles welded to each side to accommodate four to six officers who rammed the steel face of the pipe into the center of the door. It was guaranteed to open most doors.

However, in the new crack houses, the suspects learned to steel plate the doors. The LAPD solved this problem with the use of the department's new RAM.

The RAM looked like a Sherman tank but instead of a gun sticking out the front, it had a steel plate on the end, like the "Key to the City." The RAM could punch a new door in any wall in about ten seconds. Either way, the cops always got in!

I remembered Mark Allen telling us about dope dealers during roll call in the old Central Division. He warned the young rookies and the old salts to be aware of temptation. He cautioned us on what he called, the "Five Earthly P's." Mark said they were the desire for **POSITION, POSSESSIONS, POWER, POPULARITY and PLEASURE.** He wanted us to make decisions based on principles, not expedience, and routinely warned us to resist temptation.

Dope cops always have to be careful to ensure the utmost of integrity in every investigation. The "slime ball" dope dealer will lie, cheat, steal and try anything to get good cops to become bad cops. The officer must deal with those at the bottom of the pit, the snakes in the grass, the scum of the earth, and they must maintain integrity, which is the opposite of corruption.

Narcotics assignments always require the closest of scrutiny. The selection process is brutal. Probably, the great weakness is experienced after the officer is selected, when he has relatively very little supervision. Also, the cop's supervisor has a desire to be accepted by the troops. That is one reason why management must select the cream of the crop for these sensitive assignments; but, even with the tough selection process, occasionally the Five Earthly P's override the decision-making process. When this happens, the result is police corruption.

In one case, the dope cops confiscated what was supposed to be $450,000 in narcotics related cash. One narcotics officer made the property report to book the money. Three others counted the money separately and packaged it, placing their seal to certify the contents. At the end, the narcotics officer writing the reports completed the property report showing the $450,000, to be booked in as evidence. A little later, one of the dope cops doing the counting came up with an extra twenty-dollar bill, over and above the $450,000.

The cop who found the extra twenty-dollar bill went to the phone and ordered from Domino's Pizza. He had it delivered to the station. The dishonest cop paid for the pizza with the twenty-dollar bill which included a generous tip for the delivery man. As the narcotics team began to eat the delicious pizza, the officer who had used the unlawfully obtained twenty-dollar bill, told his peers what had happened. At this point, it was an unpopular decision to tell the truth and reverse the incident.

Several weeks later, it was a similar scenario, except in this case one of the officers intentionally kept two twenty-dollar bills. This time it was a better party after work in Eliasion Park. This time not only pizza, but a case of beer, was added to the menu.

Later, little corruption became big corruption. Instead of pizza and beer, it became cars, trucks, boats and even homes. Either way, little or big, both were corruption.

My friends Dick Foster and Don Stevens were both now assigned to LAPD's Narcotics Group. Note, it was a group, not a division, which meant it had a commander in charge, instead of a captain. Big deal, I thought.

Both Dick and Don loved to tell dope stories. Quite frankly, I got tired of hearing them. Or, did I?

The LAPD had loaned eight dope cops to work for a multiagency narcotics task force. The task force naturally had an acronym for a name. It was SOS-NET, for Seek Out Sources - Narcotic Enforcement Team. The SOS-NET was the brainchild of the chiefs that made up the forty-nine independent police departments in Los Angeles County and the sheriff of Los Angeles County.

SOS-NET was the result of strategic planning that took place at a week-long conference in Las Vegas, at the city's expense. Most of the planning had taken place on the golf course or during the many social hours. The chiefs came up with a plan and put it into action. The Los Angeles Police chief did not attend the conference.

LAPD usually got all the glory in large narcotics busts. The other forty-eight chiefs saw the SOS-NET as a way to be recognized and strip the LAPD chief of some of his visibility, or "glory," as they saw it.

Also, SOS-NET was a way to get their fair share of the much sought after asset forfeiture funds. This meant the police departments would get lots of dope money that was forfeited under federal law. This would give the respective chiefs money to implement their pet projects without fighting with the city manager or city council.

Asset forfeiture money was like winning the Lottery. Free money. It was easy to get, but the best part of it was that only the dope dealer got hurt.

Was it Mark Allen or Saint Paul who said, "The love of money is the root of all evil?" Or, was it both of them? The anesthetic really hit me hard, but the dreams continued.

SOS-NET really was a good idea, but control was a problem. Now the forty-eight chiefs could fight one another for control and how to make the split of the jackpot, the asset forfeiture money.

Finally, a formula was developed giving a percentage of the cut for an equal percentage of the work force. Simply stated, if one hundred narcotics officers were assigned to SOS-NET and two were from the Long Beach Police Department, that department would get two percent of the assets forfeited.

Once the formula was agreed upon by twenty-five or more of the forty-nine chiefs, then LAPD jumped in and fought to gain control of SOS-NET. No one else had the personnel resources except the Sheriff's Department. However, the sheriff never wanted to upset the Los Angeles Police chief, because the sheriff of Los Angeles County ran for reelection every four years.

Besides, some police departments viewed the Sheriff's Department as primarily a prisoner transportation and custody department. The deputies working patrol in contract cities helped boost the Sheriff's Department image and recruit young jailers. Many thought the young jailers really signed on to eventually be street cops.

Later on, LAPD got an amendment to the formula which would give a big bonus for helicopters, dope-sniffing dogs and the like. The forty-eight other chiefs called it "The Super Cop Bonus," but they never said it directly to the Los Angeles Police chief. Gutless wonders! The forty-eight were as jealous as they could be of the L. A. Police chief, who always got national attention.

Anyway, LAPD always seemed to get its fair share of everything. Their criminal intelligence file gave them a great advantage over everyone else. As an example, during just about any given year in the United States, there were nearly twelve hundred wiretaps authorized under the federal wiretap law. The LAPD would normally get nearly five percent of all the authorizations.

The Los Angeles Police Department had the expertise and the specialists to get the job done. Just think about how many hundreds of thousands of law enforcement officers there are in the United States. Los Angeles has fewer than ten thousand sworn officers to do an unbelievably difficult job.

As I lay on the couch at our cozy Lake Arrowhead home, with the fireplace crackling, the San Francisco 49ers scored a great touchdown. Things were just too comfortable, so Marie pulled the old milk request again.

Marie said, "Honey, will you run down to Cory's Market and get us a quart of milk for breakfast?"

I thought: Hon, after thirty years of marriage, why don't you start buying milk by the gallon, or at least, the half gallon. I thought it, but wisely didn't say it.

Instead, I replied, "I would love to!"

With that, I jumped up from the couch, and to make my point, turned off the TV. If I couldn't see the last two minutes of the football game, why should she? That delivered the message!

As I got in the car, I slammed the door and drove out quickly. As I headed eastbound, I immediately cooled off when realizing she didn't mean I had to leave before the game was over. Maybe I acted unreasonably on the matter. Maybe, just a little. As I headed to Cory's Market, some three miles away, I still protested the trip to myself. When I was about a half of a football field from Highway 163 and Mountain Road, a bright yellow pick-up truck, traveling westbound down the steep hill, ran the stop sign, turned right, and continued southbound on Highway 163. He was going so fast, he nearly missed the sharp right turn.

I couldn't believe this guy blew the stop sign, directly in front of me. This was an unlit, dark, rural intersection. If I had jumped off the couch before the 49ers scored, this guy would have T-boned me on the passenger side of my car.

Then, quickly I realized there was an unmarked police unit of some type, in hot pursuit of the truck. The plain unit driver had his red light and siren on as he pursued, but he was at least 100 yards behind the truck when the truck driver blew the stop sign and made the unsafe turn.

The police vehicle looked like one of the old metro units from the LAPD. But, that was impossible, with us over 100 miles from the nearest L. A. city limit sign. Then it flashed in my mind that it had to be a narcotics unit probably chasing a suspect.

They couldn't be an LAPD narcotics unit, because we always used a black and white, where possible, to stop the suspects. L. A. did it this way so the suspects couldn't say they thought it was a bad guy trying to stop them. The black and whites, with a uniform officer inside, always took away any doubt and reduced city liability.

As I looked straight ahead, with my headlights now on bright, I could see one man in the rear of the truck throwing out what appeared to be three or four boxes. The boxes were a little larger than the size of a box of copy paper.

As ·I watched I realized the truck was Hector's, the Lake Arrowhead handy man. Everyone in this small community knew him and his bright yellow pick-up truck. Hector worked all over the mountain and had a crew to rake the pine needles, fix sprinklers, and haul the debris away.

It was known that Hector always wanted cash for work performed, instead of a check. Once, I tried to give him a check for work. He responded with, "I'll come back tomorrow, so I can get the cash."

Another thing, he never gave customers a receipt for any work he did. A cop reads right through this in about ten seconds. I always thought Hector was a little shaky, but he worked cheap, so I used him as did everyone else on the mountain. This man was five-foot-four inches tall, weighed about 150 pounds, wore dark-rimmed glasses and always wore dirty blue jeans and a western shirt with those pointed pocket flaps that snap. He topped off his outfit with a straw-type, western hat.

It was rumored that Hector had an extended family in Mexico and he was sending money via Western Union to care for his family, including his elderly mother and father. That was one reason he probably wanted cash as Western Union didn't want checks.

Hector was the tobacco industry's best success story. He should have been named Joe Camel, instead of Hector. Never, did I see Hector when he didn't have a cigarette lit. He really got to me by burning the cigarette down to about a half an inch. I never figured out how he could inhale without burning his long moustache, or his finger, when he took it out of his mouth.

I had seen Hector a hundred times but, this time, I didn't see the driver of the pick-up truck. However, in that split second, my thirty-year police instinct said Hector would be behind the wheel. My instincts were usually correct, I thought.

Before the truck got out of sight, as it made its way up the curved mountain highway, the man in the back of the truck was hanging on for dear life. The tarp was blowing in the wind and leaves were flying all over the place. A good littering violation if nothing else. I would have bet the man in the back of the truck was Hector's right-hand man, Antonio.

Everything was moving as if in slow motion. Only five to ten seconds had elapsed since the truck blew past the stop sign. The police unit did the same, as they pursued the truck. By now, I was stopped about fifteen feet from the intersection and the officers in pursuit barely negotiated the right turn, also blowing past the stop sign.

As I slowly pulled across the intersection, I could not see the box near the ditch to my left. So, I continued southbound to the location where I thought the other two boxes had landed. This was about seventy or eighty feet farther south of the intersection. The road still had leaves on it that had blown out of the back of the truck.

Creeping slowly in my car, I put two and two together. The boxes probably contained marijuana, cocaine, or maybe, heroin. The cops in the unmarked unit were undoubtedly undercover narcs, and Hector and Antonio were probably dope dealers. I knew something was suspicious about Hector.

I reached under my seat and retrieved my nine-millimeter Smith and Wesson, and stuck it in my waistband, as I used to do.

Then a thought came into my mind. The narcotic officers probably never saw the suspects throw the boxes out of the truck because of their distance from the truck and their location at the time the boxes were thrown. The truck was around the corner while the officer's car was up the hill to the right, east of the intersection.

Of course, they didn't see the boxes being thrown in the ditch. If I had not started the "milk run" at the exact moment I jumped up from the couch, I would not have seen the boxes, either.

I now remembered before I stormed out of the house, I did not pick up the cell phone that was in the charging cradles on the kitchen counter. Constantly, I had yelled at Marie for not taking her cell phone when she had gone to the store.

Often I had told Marie, as well as many of our friends, the cell phone was better than carrying a concealed weapon. It is a lifeline. It is better than a police radio, because you can call anyone, not just the police, with a request for help. If I hadn't been such a jerk when asked to get the quart of milk, I'd have my cell phone with me, but I didn't. So what now?

Should I haul the boxes to the termination of the pursuit? Of course I would feel stupid if I got stopped with the boxes in the car. Or, if I had an accident, how would I ever explain such a large amount of dope in my car? After all, I was retired, or supposed to be.

Should I haul the boxes to the police station and have the boxes booked separately from the pursuit caper, then let the detectives connect the two incidents on paper, so as not to mess up the chain of continuity of evidence?

Or, should I just sit at the location, freeze my eyes on the boxes in order to maintain the continuity of evidence? Then I would wait for some citizen to come by, flag then down, ID myself as the fuzz that wuz, which didn't impress anyone.

This new role was really the pits, so I said aloud, "Let's do it." I pulled forward to the location where the two boxes appeared to have been thrown. This was farther south of the intersection than I originally thought. Driving past the right portion of the ditch where the boxes were supposed to be, I pulled my car as close to the right side as possible.

Most of my car was off the pavement in the dirt, just to the left of the ditch, but who cared? In this area of the mountains, I could park here and never see a car, here or at the intersection, for at least a half-hour.

However, instinctively, I turned on my emergency flashing lights, as I had no police lights. I grabbed my flashlight from under my front seat, just next to where I normally hid my nine-millimeter automatic. I pushed the trunk release button, left my car running and jumped out of my new Ford just as I did thirty years earlier on the Harbor Freeway, when the Wade's Gun Store caper went down. Somehow, this incident tonight made me feel younger.

With my flashlight, I could see two of the boxes very clearly. I grabbed the sealed boxes, one at a time because they were rather heavy, and threw them into the trunk of my car. I slammed the trunk lid, and made an illegal U-turn with my emergency lights still flashing. This felt good!

As I drove north back toward the intersection, I looked frantically for the first box that was thrown. I clearly had seen the box hit the asphalt highway then take a couple of bounces before it hit the ditch. This was not going to be fun. The weeds in the ditch were high. There was probably water in the bottom.

I even suspected that I would find snakes in the bottom of the ditch. I hated snakes and would bet if I had to go to the bottom of the shallow ditch, I'd find them.

With my flashlight, I continued to search the area when I spotted the first box that was thrown. It apparently had bounced to the west side of the ditch, closer to the intersection than I thought. This time, I didn't pull to the right. I just blocked the lane, jumped out, hopped over the ditch and got the box.

As I had not popped the trunk lid, I tried the back right passenger door, but of course it was locked. When I entered the driver's door, I pushed the box into the passenger side of the front seat.

The boxes had been wrapped with duct tape and were really heavy, much heavier than they looked. The duct tape was the type my air conditioning man had used to wrap the air condition ducts at our Palm Springs home. Expensive tape, I thought.

Then, I pulled forward into the intersection, my flashers still on, and whipped another U-turn to head for the direction of the pursuit.

As I started moving south on Highway 163, I clicked the interior light on for the first time.

Part of the tape on this box had been torn and one corner was crushed in. The box looked as if it had an indentation on it from skidding on the rough asphalt.

Had Marie been with me, she would have protested my placing the dirty box on her seat in the car. However, because the seats were leather, I could clean off all the crud from the dirty box by simply wiping off the seat with a wet cloth. She would never know.

As I continued slowly, southbound on 163, in the direction of the pursuit, I began to examine the box next to me. It had 4.7 written on each side with a felt tip pen. The numbers were about two inches tall. Maybe this was a lot number for the shipment of dope, then I laughed to myself. Whoever heard of dope with lot numbers? They did not want it to be identifiable.

Maybe, the 4.7 had to do with the weight of the contents of the box. It might mean forty-seven pounds. I would estimate the weight of the box to be about fifty pounds. Maybe fifty to a hundred pounds.

Then I thought, Give me a break. How do I know what fifty pounds feels like? I didn't have calibrated muscles or eyeballs.

By the time I had traveled about a mile, I was at the Mountain Congregational Church, so I made a left turn into the church parking lot. I was still curious about what I was hauling to the officers in the pursuit.

As I rolled the box over, the dented corner with the frayed tape had a slight rip in it. Obviously, it was damaged from the way it had hit the pavement. I did my part to disturb the evidence, and put my curiosity to rest. I tore the box portion back about six inches, where the tape was already frayed.

It looked like an old Ford radiator core, but the contents were paper, not lead, brass or other metals. I tore the box about another three inches, to try to satisfy my curiosity.

Then I said to myself, "Brad Phillips, can you believe this?" I could not believe my eyes. I really expected marijuana, wrapped in kilos, but it was paper. From what I could tell, the paper was stacked very tightly in the box. The strips of paper were about two and a half inches in width, and were green in color. Green like money.

At that moment, in the middle of the Mountain Congregational Church parking lot, I turned off my flashers, headlights and inside dome light. I just froze. I just sat there for several minutes. Now, I concluded that Hector and Antonio were "mules." They were money mules and were probably hauling the money to buy the dope.

While sitting there, I heard sirens approaching my location. I expected to see several black and white police units going to backup the officers in the pursuit. I was wrong. It was three fire trucks heading in the direction of the pursuit, southbound on Highway 163. The fire trucks appeared to be coming from the Blue Jay Area. Why from Blue Jay instead of the units in Cedar Glen? Oh well, maybe an unrelated matter.

I didn't think the fire units saw me, as all my lights were out. After they were long gone, I again started toward the direction of the pursuit. As I crossed the dam at the head of the lake, just before entering Cedar Glen, I saw a huge ball of fire and heard what sounded like a sonic boom. It looked like a jet had crashed near Cory's Market.

Speeding up, I followed the fire and smoke, which were in the same direction of the pursuit. As I approached Cory's Market, I could see why the fire units had come all the way from Blue Jay. They had about ten fire units from all over the mountain by the time I got there. A vehicle had apparently crashed into the Cedar Glen Chevron station, next to Cory's Market.

Apparently, the first fire units at the scene were from Cedar Glen. Then, fire units from Lake Arrowhead Village arrived, before the Blue Jay units responded. Fires are a great source of concern in the mountains, so firefighters always jump on fires quickly, like stink on a skunk.

There were already a couple of black and white police units directing traffic. Because they had not passed me, they obviously had come from the south, traveling northbound, the opposite direction around the lake and the opposite direction of the pursuit.

Traffic could no longer travel north or south on Highway 163. It was blocked, so I pulled my car into Cory's parking lot. I grabbed my jacket off the back seat, and draped it over the box in my front passenger seat. I stuck my gun and flash light back under the seat where they belonged. I got out, locked the doors with my remote door locker and figured I would have to wait until Highway 163 opened up. Then I'd find the dope cops and the end of the pursuit.

So as to keep peace in the family, I went in the market and purchased a quart of milk, as directed. This time, I checked the date on the front carton, then pulled one from the rear. Sure enough, it had a later date, by one day. My wife would be proud of me. When I got to the small check out stand, the young clerk's eyes were glued on the fire and excitement outside. Then I thought, she probably had never seen a big fire. For that matter, maybe not even a little fire.

I'd seen plenty of fires, some where the fire had left nothing but "crispy critter." I'd seen it and did not like the sight or thought of it.

I remembered the incident where four young men, all under twenty-one years old, had been burned so badly, yet lived for one, four, sixteen and twenty-two days, respectively after a meth-lab exploded. The bad part was interviewing them immediately after the explosion.

Each one of the young men could talk, but they were in shock. Their lungs were fried and they looked like a cooked animal. It was the worst I'd ever seen and I would never get that investigation out of my mind. I believed anyone who worked in such horror such as the firemen, had earned a tax-free pension. So I was just going to conceal my true feelings, be a good boy and buy the quart of milk.

As I walked to my car, I unlocked the door and placed the sack with the milk on the driver's side. Again, I locked the door, to maintain the continuity of evidence, and walked toward the uniformed officer assigned to direct what little traffic might appear. As I got closer, I saw the undercover unit from the pursuit parked on the other side of three fire trucks.

The firefighters were still trying to get a handle on the fire, but were a long way away from gaining control. It did look like a jet airplane had crashed into the gas station. There had to be "crispy critters" involved, but I really did not want to see them.

As I got closer to the uniformed officer, I said, "Officer, where are the officers in that undercover unit," as I pointed. The officer was looking toward the fire, with his back toward me. I was ignored, so I repeated the same statement. With that, the officer turned around and rudely said, "Get out of here, can't you see the fire." I then noticed, he had apparently been talking on his police radio when I was asking him where the other officers were.

I responded, "I'm sorry, but I'm a retired..." With that, he threw his microphone down on the seat, and yelled at me and pointed his finger toward the sidewalk in front of Cory's Market and said, "I don't care who you are, get back on the sidewalk, or I'll book you."

Retirement was hard to adjust to, but this guy absolutely humiliated me in front of the two clerks from the store, who were now outside watching the fire. I was embarrassed, humiliated and felt sick from the smell of burnt bodies.

As I tucked my tail between my legs and walked back to the curb, I passed by the fire hydrant, where a fire fighter was now stationed. He had heard me getting chewed out by some cop who had probably never taken the "How to Talk to the Public" class at the L. A. Police Academy. Or, was he as uneasy with the burning body, or bodies, as I was?

Maybe he had not been trained as effectively as I had, to conceal his true emotions. Or, maybe, it was better for him to vent his feelings. No one liked seeing "crispy critters." I was embarrassed to say anything to the veteran firefighter, but I swallowed my pride and asked him what happened. To my surprise, he had plenty of time and liked to talk. I guess his job was turning the valve on and off. What a job, I thought.

The firefighter said narcotic officers were pursuing a truck toward Lake Arrowhead Village when the truck decided to take a short cut, not a pit stop, through the gas station. A car started to pull away from the pump and the truck swerved to miss it and sheered off a couple of the gas pumps. When this happened there was an explosion and the place went up like a bomb hit it.

I asked, "What type of a truck was it? How many were in the truck?"

The fireman pointed to the fire, and said, "If we ever get this fire out, you won't know it was a truck. We probably won't even be able to count bodies. That fire is hotter than a crematorium."

I just responded with, "Huh!" and walked slowly back to my car. I got in the car and verified the evidence, or found property, on my front passenger seat under my jacket, was still secure. Then I slowly drove home.

When I got home I pulled into the garage, closed the door and took the one box from the front passenger seat and placed it in the trunk, so as to retain the continuity of evidence. After retrieving the quart of milk from the car, I put it on the top shelf in the refrigerator.

Marie was already dressed for bed when I went upstairs to the bedroom. She was sitting up in bed with a book in her hand.

Marie said, "Brad, I was really worried about you. After you left, there were lots of sirens in the area. I was afraid something had happened to you. I tried to call you on your cell phone but then I saw that you had left it in the kitchen."

I replied, "I forgot the phone, so don't bug me about it anymore. There was a big accident at the Cedar Glen Chevron. A fireman told me the truck involved in the accident burned up with whoever, or whatever, was in the truck. You know how I feel about burnt bodies. I got the milk and put it in the refrigerator."

Marie started to ask me more about why I didn't take the cell phone and about the incident.

I concluded the conversation with a cold comment, "Enough about the fire!"

As I lay in bed, I could not sleep. Thoughts raced through my mind. I tossed and turned. Marie and my psychologist were the only two people in this world, other than myself, who knew my true emotions and feelings about "crispy critters." She knew very well how I felt on the subject, so maybe that is why she was giving me a break on the fact I didn't take the cell phone with me to the store.

Three times during the night, I got up very quietly and returned to the trunk of my car. I didn't use the remote trunk opener that beeped, but quietly used my key.

Marie knew I was getting up, but I figured she was again letting me work the "crispy critter" memory out in my own way. She knew me backward and forward, but she didn't know my trunk was loaded with evidence, or found property.

15

FOUND PROPERTY

Just before 6 a.m., I shook Marie, who was finally falling asleep. She was out of it. I had kept her awake most of the night by getting up and checking the evidence locked in the trunk of my car. Marie had not been put through such a night since just after the fire at the meth-lab, three years earlier, when the four young men were fatally burned. Marie had stuck with me through the entire traumatic ordeal.

During the night I had taken a razor blade and carefully slit open the box marked 4.7. I was careful not to disturb the evidence. I knew, without a doubt, the box was not full of twenty-dollar bills as I had suspected. It wasn't even fifty-dollar bills. Every bill I could see was a hundred-dollar bill. I could not find any ones, fives, tens, twenties or fifties. They were all one-hundred-dollar bills. Unbelievable!

It was impossible to estimate how many would be in the box. I assumed the other two boxes contained the same. Or, there could be different denominations in each box. I really didn't want to disturb the evidence by opening up the others.

My mind flashed back to the narcotic officers who had started their corruption with a single twenty-dollar bill to buy a pizza.

Marie was still fighting to get her sleep as I tossed around. Suddenly I shook her and told her, "I do not want you to argue or discuss my decision. Let's just get up!"

Of course she said, "What decision?" She then looked at me as if I was crazy.

I told her we needed to get up immediately and go to our desert home. She didn't like it, but I figured she thought I was having problems with the "crispy critter" thing.

For the first time in our thirty years of marriage I said we didn't have time to shower. After a lot of protest she finally threw her white sweatsuit outfit on and headed for the car. She did not like what I was doing and it showed on her face and in her actions.

I closed up the mountain house while she sat in the car. She leaned her seat back and tried to fall asleep again.

Without saying a word, I backed out of the driveway and headed toward the desert by way of Cedar Glen, the same route of the pursuit and fire. Marie raised herself up and asked, "Why are you going this way?"

We always went the opposite way around the lake when we left because it was closer, but my response to Marie was, "I thought you might like to see the fire damage."

I wanted to see what was left after the fire. I wanted to retrace the route. I wanted to see if there was a fourth, fifth or sixth box lying in the ditch between Mountain Bay Road and the Chevron station. Besides, I wanted to be the first car traveling to Cedar Glen on Highway 163. I had my reasons.

I drove slowly this morning. Although Marie was trying to sleep, she sat up and asked what I was doing. She knew I hadn't driven slowly since I got my driver's license at age sixteen. This was totally out of character for me.

Although she didn't say it, Marie had to be wondering what I was doing going by and looking at what remained of the fire. She knew what it had done to me in the past.

I could not spot any more boxes on or near the road or ditch. My eyes searched both sides like a man with a pair of binoculars at a beauty contest, or a man lighting a cigarette in a topless bar. But this search was more important. I had to make a decision soon!

As we passed Cory's Market I shook Marie and she sat up. Things were very quiet at the Chevron station. The firefighter who had worked the fire hydrant last night was right. There wasn't much left on the lot, except the yellow crime scene tape around the perimeter. Everyone was gone. It was quiet as I passed. I told Marie, I had not seen a fire like this one since the Watts Riots. She looked at me and said, "How about the meth-lab?" If she had gotten a good night's sleep, she would not have said that. She was just tired. I knew her like a book!

Down the mountain we went. Less than two hours later we were at our other home. This time, I never went over the speed limit and I didn't do any changing back and forth in the lanes. Simply, I didn't want to get stopped by the CHP or have an accident while hauling the evidence, or found property.

When we got to the house, I pulled into the garage and immediately closed the door. Marie stared at me but didn't say a word until she got out of the car and discovered the dirt she had on the seat of her white outfit. I had forgotten to clean the seat and she wasn't happy.

We walked into the house and sat down in the living room after I got a towel for her to cover the chair she had to sit in. We never used the living room, so she knew this was serious business.

Before she met me, Marie had lived a pretty clean and simple life. Her folks lived in the same house for sixty-five years and her father had driven a Studebaker. They were very stable and she was easy to please.

She had just three "vices." She would give the shirt off her back, and mine for that matter, to our boys, and never blink an eye. She really loved those kids. Two, she thought I was a good and honest man. She would stick with me no matter what, through thick or thin. Three, she liked designer shoes. She had forty-nine pairs. They were all stacked like a shoe store in the closet. The shoe boxes were replaced with plastic storage containers that were a little larger and took up a little more space. She purchased them at Target for two dollars each.

Her pure, simple and honest ways of living had earned her the title of "Saint Marie" from some of our friends, but this morning I thought, not in this life, now we are going to be rich. Real rich!

We never kept secrets from each other. I had to tell her. So, I told her the whole story and didn't leave anything out. She looked at me as though I was describing a dream. For the next hour, I listened to her plead with me to call the police and end this thing.

My best argument was the "found property" theory. I used the technical definition, then threw in "finders keepers," but she didn't bite.

Marie was quick to point out that I had seen the man in the back of the truck actually throw the boxes from the truck. She went on with something such as, "Yeah, Bradley, they just dropped down from the sky, right in front of you, as you went to Cory's to buy milk." She wasn't stupid. She had graduated from USC with honors and had taught school for twenty-plus years.

Next, I told her my dislike for dope dealers and how destructive they were. I gave the DARE pitch that I once used to raise money for the program. Keeping the money was taking the profit out of crime, much like asset forfeiture laws provided. This was a weak argument and I knew it.

Then, I tried the "no-witness" theory, which didn't work much better. I emphasized that probably no one had seen me before, during or after I put the found property in my trunk. She said it was evidence, I said it was found property, without a known owner. I argued that if I found the original dope dealer, it would be better for us to keep it than return it to him.

Then I made the mistake of pleading with her to let me buy a new Cessna-182 that I had always wanted, or maybe a twin-engine Baron. Wrong! I probably sounded like a kid in a candy store asking for more candy.

Marie could care less about an airplane. The expression on her face told me I was dreaming if I thought she would ever go for that.

Finally, I worked in the marriage vows about, "for better or worse," "for richer or poorer" and "do it my way or no way." She didn't recall the latter part. Then, I lost control and ended up with something such as "My way or the highway." I'm sure she thought the fire had flipped me out.

She began to cry. I put my arm around her and assured her everything was going to be okay. Then I kissed her, as though I was just going through the motions.

I went to the garage and found my new lightweight, bright blue, eight-foot-by-ten-foot plastic tarp. I took this into our master bedroom. It had never been opened. I closed all the black-out curtains, turned on the lights and spread the tarp on the floor.

Marie was still sitting in the living room with her head in her hands. She was probably praying. I gave her space and quickly brought in all three boxes, spacing them neatly on the tarp along the ten-foot edge. The room was prepared like a money count in a police property room: neat and clean.

Trying to get Marie with me on the matter, I went to the living room and said, "Come on, Honey, I hereby deputize you. Come help me count this money."

Counting the money was like playing a big Monopoly game on the floor when the boys were young. Except, this was for real, I thought.

It took us an hour and a half to finish the first box, which contained four hundred seventy bundles of money. Each bundle had exactly one hundred, one-hundred-dollar bills in it. There was ten thousand dollars in each bundle. The 4.7 on the box represented $4.7 million in the first box.

Marie was not impressed, but I could not wait to open the second box with the 5.6 written on the outside. When I discovered that 5.6 meant $5.6 million, I nearly choked.

The third box had 5.3 written on it. Yep, it had $5.3 million in it. This now brought the grand total to $15.6 million and it was not even noon yet. Not bad for a day's work.

I quickly figured you would have to earn $27 million in order to have $15.6 million clear, after taxes. Marie didn't like it, but was wide awake now.

Then the problem came. The $15.6 million wouldn't fit in my small safe. I searched the garage for a container. The best I could find was an ice chest that would not hold all the money.

I went to the bedroom to discuss the matter with Marie, but she had gone to the kitchen. The closet door in the master bedroom was open and then I spotted my solution. All I needed was to get Marie to agree to let me use thirty-nine of her forty-nine storage boxes, temporarily.

"Sure. Why not?" was her reply, which really meant she didn't like it. My dumping her shoes into the ice chest for storage was a big mistake.

The $400,000 fit neatly into each of the storage boxes. I put the boxes on the floor of the closet under the clothes after nearly breaking the shelf with the boxes. I sealed each container with one strip of duct tape to prevent anyone from opening them without being obvious.

At 5:00 p.m. I asked Marie to go out for dinner. I showered, got dressed and stuck ten of the bills in my money clip and headed for La Casa Restaurant.

After a strained dinner with Marie, I paid the thirty-seven-dollar check and gave the waiter a thirteen-dollar tip, all out of a crisp one-hundred-dollar bill. En route home, I stopped at the service station

175

and fueled my car, paying the attendant the twenty-one dollars with another one-hundred bill. Naturally I had to stop at the market to pick up a quart of milk, paying for it with a one-hundred-dollar bill and then to the Lottery desk to purchase ten five-dollar Quick Picks with another one-hundred-dollar bill. Now, I had used my fourth hundred-dollar bill and I had plenty of change!

How long would it take me to spend $15.6 million at this rate? Each shoe box would last nearly three years if I spent $400 each day. At this rate the thirty-eight shoe boxes would last over a hundred years. Could that much money allow me to live that much longer? I didn't think so.

After dinner we crashed. We were so tired and exhausted, we slept until eight the next morning.

Marie was already up when I awoke. She had prepared one of those breakfasts she only cooked for company or our boys. Everything was perfect. Linen tablecloth and napkins, silver cream and sugar set, everything. I knew something was coming after breakfast. Look out!

After we finished the dishes, Marie said, as if I was to be surprised, "We have to talk." Back to the living room we went.

For an hour and a half she talked about where we came from, where we had been and where we were going. She started off with the fact that when we first got married we had nothing but each other. Everything we had acquired, we had earned through hard work, sweat and tears. We had taught our boys to base decisions on principles, not expediency.

Marie went on with how we had earned our retirement in our chosen professions and lived very comfortably. We didn't have everything, but what we had was ours and we had respect for what we did.

She concluded her plea with the fact that she would walk the face of the earth with me, she would sweep the gutter with me if necessary, but she wanted to live an honest, respectful life. She said these things were more than money.

I told her she had to give me some time to think about it. I didn't tell her, but $15.6 million took a lot of soul searching to declare it as evidence again. Found property sounded better at this moment.

Before I got back to the evidence-or-found-property decision, I wanted to figure out how I could spend the $15.6 million without getting caught.

If I spent large chunks of money on anything the IRS or State Franchise Board would swoop down on me. This eliminated houses, boats, new cars and airplanes.

Really, the only thing, over a long period of time, would be to spend the money on expendables. Very little money could be spent on nonexpendables. That is why the dope dealers get caught laundering money.

Maybe she was right. We did live relatively comfortable.

By 9:00 p.m., I walked into the bedroom hoping to put our marriage back together. The news was just beginning on the television. I put my pajamas on while she was reading her book. The reporter announced the pursuit which started over a suspected narcotics deal but no narcotics were found. They reported the two deaths, although the bodies and truck were burned beyond recognition. No mention was made of any money related to the incident.

Marie ignored the report and kept reading her book. She acted as though she didn't see or hear the televised news report.

I said, "Well, isn't that great. They didn't mention any money involved in the incident."

She only grunted with, "Uh."

With that, I said, "Good night!"

Thursday morning I got up before Marie. I picked up the paper and skimmed it. Then I couldn't believe it. For the first time in my life I had the six winning lottery numbers. All six numbers were on the same line. We had won the lottery! The jackpot was supposed to be $20 million. I quickly called the 800 number to verify the good news but I didn't want to say anything to Marie yet. I could use this to negotiate with her, maybe.

I again called the 800 number and the lottery officials verified my numbers as winners, but, to my disappointment, they advised me the pot would be split between me and the other five winners. I refused to give my name at this point and said I would call back. Winners had not split the pot in two years. But, they never had split the jackpot with six winning numbers in the history of the state's lottery.

This meant that each winner would receive $3.3 million, however I had checked the lottery ticket for cash not twenty-six payments over a twenty-six-year period.

Bottom line, this meant they would only pay me about fifty percent of the $3.3 million or about $1.6 million. They would then hold out fifty percent for the IRS and State Franchise Tax Board, netting us about $800,000 cash. It seemed so small when the jackpot was $20 million.

I called the lottery office again and asked what would happen if some of the six winners did not turn in the tickets. They confirmed it would then be split with those who claimed their winnings within sixty days. Maybe someone would lose their ticket.

When Marie got up, I told her we were winners all the way around. We had $15.6 million plus at least another $800,000 as we had been one of the six winners in the lottery. Now we had $16.4 million to spend, but it would be much easier because we didn't have to launder nearly a million dollars of the money.

She had a problem with the whole thing. Now she protested that the lottery ticket was bought with illegally obtained money and we were depriving the other five winners of their rightful share.

I could not believe it. All my dreams would go down the tube. No new airplane, no new house, no new car, no free travel, no free lunches. It was worse than a bad dream. It was like a nightmare or psycho dream.

Marie didn't care about material possessions. Character, honesty, integrity and love were her treasures. She actually wanted me to give up all the material things that I could buy.

16

OFFICER NEEDS HELP

In 1968, the LAPD formed a small task force to study the antiquated and outdated radio communication system that was being used in the city of Los Angeles. Millions of dollars went into studying the problem and for recommending solutions to the problem.

Due to lack of funding, it was not until June 1976, when the Los Angeles voters approved the tax override to build the new Emergency Command Communication Center System (ECCCS), pronounced "X" System. Thirty years later, the same task force was still functioning. The name was the same but the faces had changed. I asked myself, why would the department need this for thirty years? The answer was simple: things change.

Technology is moving so rapidly, we must change with the times. The world is a connected global community, not just our little world of yesterday.

One thing that hasn't changed is the fact that officers are still giving their lives in the line of duty, many times beyond the call of duty. Since ECCCS was formed, approximately two officers have been killed in the line of duty each year.

Before the taxpayers started voting for the necessary funds to put in the expensive upgraded systems, the street cops believed it was just a dream. They believed city government moved so slowly that, any major improvements would not occur in their professional lifetime.

The most important single radio message an L. A. street cop has is the "Officer Needs Help" call. For departments that use the radio nine series it is "999" or "11-99." They all mean the same. Officers are careful to put this message out only when in imminent danger and when their existing resources cannot handle the situation.

For less serious situations, there are requests such as "Officer Needs Assistance," "Requesting Another Unit Code 2," or simply, "Requesting a Back-up Unit," with no code designated. But when help is really needed, street cops know the call is "Officer Needs Help."

When officers hear the call, they drop whatever they are doing to help their brother or sister officer. If a traffic violator is receiving a citation, better known as a "ticket," the citizen gets a free ride. He lets the violator go free as he stops what he (or she) is doing to hurry and provide help to the officer in need.

In the early stage of ECCCS, the designers came up with a hand-held radio they named ROVER, meaning Remote Out of Vehicle Emergency Radio. This radio, which weighed less than twelve ounces, clipped onto the officer's belt and no longer restricted the officer to the police vehicle.

Radio communication provided true mobility for the officer. When the radio was inserted in the radio charger in the police vehicle it became even more powerful, giving it greater range, as it used the vehicle antenna and also charged the battery.

The radio had a button that could be activated by the officer, which was an "Officer Needs Help" signal. The word no longer had to be spoken, just push the button and help was summoned. Today, the technology is here to send and receive the "Officer Needs Help" call. Communications shows the identity of the ROVER and pinpoints the call and the location. The cost of the system was millions of dollars, but the result in saving lives was indeed worth more than money.

Over the last thirty years, the radio got lighter and more powerful. Things change.

Now the anesthetic was beginning to wear off. My chest and insides really hurt. And, I was so dopey. As I opened up my eyes I could see Marie standing next to the bed. She leaned forward and kissed me on my left cheek.

I flickered my eyes, and said, "Where am I?"

Marie answered, "Honey, you had a heart attack. I called the ambulance and they brought you to Hilltop Hospital, here in Cedar Glen. The doctor said you had to be operated on immediately. They rushed you into surgery. You've been out of the recovery room for about four hours. You are now in Room 23 and Doctor Melborne says you will be fine."

I panicked and responded with, "Is the money still in the house? In our Palm Springs home?"

Marie looked at me and responded with, "Brad, we sold the desert home when we moved to Lake Arrowhead. Don't you remember that?"

I paused and finally replied, "Yeah, that's right; I'm just joking," but I wasn't. "Have you seen Hector lately?"

Giving me a puzzled look Marie answered me with, "As a matter of fact, he and Margarita brought flowers by the house this morning. They are praying for your recovery."

I gasped, as pain shot through me, and asked weakly, "What was he driving?"

She said, "Brad, you know Hector has been driving that old dark red pick-up truck for as long as we have known him. Why do you ask?"

I muttered, "I was thinking he had a new bright yellow pick-up truck."

Marie laughed and replied, "Don't you remember? Hector, you and I had a discussion about car colors last Saturday. Hector told us he disliked bright yellow cars. That was also the day Hector told you about how he had stopped smoking twenty years ago. Bradley, don't you remember the conversation? Are you okay?"

I concluded my interrogation of Marie with one last question. "Have we ever won the California Lottery?"

Marie laughed heartily and said, "Yes. Last Saturday we had three numbers on one line. We won five dollars."

I then closed my eyes. I didn't want to dream anymore. Being alive, without a doubt, meant much more than money.

ABOUT THE AUTHOR

For thirty years, D. Clayton Mayes was a professional law enforcement officer. He began his career with the Los Angeles police department in 1964. He worked as a street cop, was promoted to investigator, sergeant, lieutenant and captain. In 1990, he retired from the LAPD to assume the responsibilities of chief of police of the Downey, (California) Police Department.

The author holds a bachelor's degree in public management and a master's degree in public administration from Pepperdine University. He is also a graduate of the FBI-National Academy in Quantico, Virginia. As an educator, he has taught at Cerritos College, College of the Desert and has instructed throughout the United States for the Federal Law Enforcement Training Center and the U.S. Department of Justice, Office of Juvenile Justice and Delinquency Prevention. He served a total of six years in the U.S. Army, Army Reserve, and the California National Guard where he attained the rank of captain.

Today Clayton lives in the Palm Springs, California, area with his wife, Carolyn. Their two sons are grown. The author enjoys golf, tennis and flying. He holds a commercial pilot license, with an instrument rating for both single-engine and multi-engine aircraft.

Printed in the United States
17467LVS00002B/1-78